"Though you can stay at a distance, this isn't where I'll stay. I plan on wallowing in this incredible thing we have."

She almost choked. "We don't have anything…"

"We do. And it's undeniable, unstoppable." H leaned to brush his firm, cool lips against the long-scorched skin at her jaw before pulling back. "And I won't be either denied or stopped. But, as I said, at your pace. My patience is legendary. Now, let's stock you up on more calories."

And for the next hour he fed her things she'd never tasted before, delicacies of his land, sharing every bite with her as he told her their names and their recipes.

She surrendered to his ministrations, the urge mounting to tell him that if the baby wasn't all that mattered, he might not have needed to be patient at all.

But as it was, no amount of patience would do him good. No matter how much she longed to, she wouldn't, *couldn't*, succumb to his annihilating temptation.

Olivia Gates has always pursued many passions. But the time came when she had to set up a 'passion priority', to give her top one her all, and writing won. Hands down. She is most fulfilled when she is creating worlds and conflicts for her characters and then exploring and untangling them bit by bit, sharing her protagonists' every heartache and hope and heart-pounding doubt until she leads them to their indisputably earned and glorious happy ending. When she's not writing she is a doctor, a wife to her own alpha male, and a mother to one brilliant girl and one demanding Angora cat.

Please visit Olivia at http://www.oliviagates.com

Recent titles by the same author:

THE SHEIKH SURGEON'S PROPOSAL
THE SURGEON'S RUNAWAY BRIDE
THE HEROIC SURGEON
THE DOCTOR'S LATIN LOVER

DESERT PRINCE, EXPECTANT MOTHER

BY
OLIVIA GATES

MILLS & BOON®
Pure reading pleasure™

First published in Great Britain 2008
Large Print edition 2008
Harlequin Mills & Boon Limited,
Eton House, 18-24 Paradise Road,
Richmond, Surrey TW9 1SR

ISBN: 978 0 263 19985 7

Set in Times Roman 16 on 17¾ pt.
17-1008-56944

Printed and bound in Great Britain
by Antony Rowe Ltd, Chippenham, Wiltshire

DESERT PRINCE, EXPECTANT MOTHER

To my husband and daughter.
For making it possible for me to
keep on dreaming, to keep on writing.

To my editor, Sheila Hodgson.
For making both activities increasingly
enjoyable and rewarding.

CHAPTER ONE

LARISSA MCPHERSON was a woman in full control of her faculties, by nature, by necessity, and by vocation.

Or so she'd thought.

Anybody watching her right now would surmise that she had as much self-possession as an empty-headed, starstruck schoolgirl.

If anybody had told her when she'd arrived in Bidalya yesterday that when she headed to Az-Zufranah Royal Medical Complex the first thing she'd do would be to make a fool of herself she wouldn't have considered that worth a reply.

As it turned out, it hadn't been the first thing she'd done.

She'd first walked into the town-sized complex and let Reception know she'd arrived for her first day of work. In a minute a young woman heralded by a cloud of perfume and a toothpaste-model smile had come rushing to meet her, extending a ringed, painted-in-intricate-henna-patterns hand to her. Larissa had extended her hand, expecting a handshake, only to find herself dragged into an enthusiastic embrace and kissed once on the right cheek and twice on the left.

Stepping back from the energetic greeting, Larissa had found out Soha was another of the ultra-affable personnel organizing the executive side of the project she was here to join, those who'd turned her every minute on Bidalyan soil so far into a flawless dream. Soha told her someone would come immediately to escort her on a tour of the complex and to hand her her responsibilities for the three months she was here for.

She hadn't been able to help feeling self-conscious as she'd watched the vivacious Soha walking away. Compared to the stunning, haute couture-clad Bidalyan women she'd seen so far—those who weren't covered from head to toe, that was—she'd been feeling decidedly dowdy with her utilitarian clothes, scrubbed-clean face and practical ponytail.

Shaking her head at the unfamiliar longing for a more sophisticated exterior, telling herself that she'd never pull off these women's ultra-sleek look and couldn't afford to invest the time and effort in achieving it anyway, she'd turned around.

And she'd seen him. Prowling from the far end

of one of the street-wide, mirror-marble corridors opening into the cathedral-huge reception area, flanked by people who'd been running to keep up with his long strides. And she'd no longer been able to see anything else. Then he'd turned his gaze in her direction and something had speared into her gut and rooted her legs to the spot.

She now stood mesmerized, watching his graceful and power-laden motion, her heart hammering, her hands clammy, a current buzzing from her armpits down to her toes. She swallowed. Again.

Oh, man. Her mouth was actually watering. Worse, she just knew anybody looking at her could tell that it was. Starting with him. Then it got worse still. She could swear everything had decelerated, like one of those slow-motion scenes that emphasized dramatic moments in movies, as if to mark the gravity of his presence, the enormity of his approach.

Which was a totally stupid thing to be thinking. Not to mention a far more stupid way to be feeling.

What was wrong with her? The hyperbole, the electricity, the breath that had shuddered out of her and now couldn't be drawn in again? It was as if she'd never seen an incredible-looking guy before.

Problem was, she'd seen tons. But that man certainly wasn't one. It would be an insult to call him anything so run-of-the-mill. He had the aura of a mystical knight, with power enough to bear mythic burdens, determination enough to forge legends. Had a face to make angels weep and a body to make the gods of old fade into insignificance…

This had gotten beyond ridiculous. She had to be having some sort of breakdown, imagining all those far-fetched things about a man who was still two dozen feet away.

But she was becoming surer he'd end up addressing her.

She dreaded it. And hoped for it. He'd probably smash the illusion with the first word he uttered. Maybe before that. She'd surely come to her senses with one good look into his eyes. She was bound to see all the flaws a male of this level of beauty invariably harbored, all the superficiality, the egocentricity. He'd probably put her off with his first presumptuous, self-satisfied smirk. And it wouldn't be a second too soon.

She couldn't afford any sort of distraction. She was here in Bidalya for a specific purpose, with the surgical trainer job she'd signed up for the means to her being here long enough to carry it out. She was here only to find out all she could about the family of the baby she was carrying!

The last thing she needed in the equation now, on her mind, interfering with her clarity of analysis and decisions, was a man. Any man. And when it was a man of this caliber…she couldn't even chart the possible damages.

OK. This had gone way beyond ridiculous. Beyond deranged. All these scenarios when the man had done nothing but look at her, head her way. He might look away at any moment, might not even stop anywhere near her, let alone talk to her. This *must* be her first taste of wayward early pregnancy hormones.

But the next second other sets of hormones were going ballistic.

The man was now a few feet away, and the slowed-down effect deepened, as if time was caught in a frame-by-frame sequence in awe of his proximity, to do his impending arrival justice.

He *was* looking at her, with an intensity and focus that penetrated her bones. He *was* going to talk to her. But it wasn't that knowledge that sent tremors storming through her. It was the awareness, the sensuality that flamed in the depths of those obsidian eyes. It was knowing she'd invited them with her runaway and blatant reaction.

For God's sake, look away.

She couldn't. His mesmeric power was something she'd never had any experience with, had no defenses against. Then he finally stopped, too close…

She felt she was suffocating. Her chest tightened, her vision began to blotch. She gulped down an oxygen-starved breath, nearly choked. She'd breathed him in. She couldn't breathe without breathing him in, his maleness, his dominance. She gulped it all down, felt it all rush to her core.

His eyes flared on a last probing, ascertaining her reaction, his welcome. Then they grew heavy with knowing, with promise as he inhaled the breath that preceded the first words. She wished she could block her ears, talk first, run away, do anything so she wouldn't hear him, loath to destroy the illusion, scared it wouldn't destroy it, would only deepen the spell.

"Who…?"

He didn't go any further. A shout ripped the air, sent both of them spinning around to its source.

"Dr. Faress."

A man was running towards them, urgency written all over him.

So her mystery man was a doctor. And his name was Faress. She got this. It meant knight in Arabic. This kept on getting worse.

What she didn't get was one word of the torrent

of colloquial Arabic the man deluged Dr. Faress with. But there was no mistaking the gravity of the report he was relaying.

She did a double take as she watched the dramatic change that came over Dr. Faress's face. The sensuality and curiosity that had melted his gaze and ripened his lips evaporated, purpose replacing it, tautening his features and expression over the perfection of his bone structure.

In a few words he sent the messenger running back then turned to her, his gaze still intense, if devoid of the intimate fire that had burned in their depths moments before. So he was capable of switching off on demand, of prioritizing.

"Tell me who you are." It was a demand. Almost an order. And it felt neither presumptuous nor offensive. Not coming from him.

"I-I'm Dr. Larissa McPherson." She was genuinely surprised she could still talk. She wished *he* hadn't. Instead of shattering the illusion, the depth and richness of his tones, the darkness and potency of his accent, the virile beauty of his every inflection deepened her distress. She somehow managed to add, "I'm new here."

His spectacular winged eyebrows drew closer in the frown of someone trying to place a name and failing. "New here doing what?"

"I'm with the training program the complex is sponsoring."

God, she sounded like an idiot. And could she have been more vague? A place of such resources could, and must be, sponsoring dozens of training programs.

Sure enough, he tried to drag something more specific from her. Amazingly he got warm, if not spot on, on the first try. "You're one of Global Aid Organization's volunteer trainees?"

"No, I'm one of the surgical trainers."

"You're a surgeon?"

Now, this was his first unnecessary question. She'd said she was a surgical trainer. What else could she be? A hairdresser?

Yet she knew it had been a rhetorical question, an exclamation.

And she couldn't blame him for his stupefaction. Capable surgeons who'd been picked as surgical trainers didn't drool over men—no matter how godlike—on sight, and they didn't stammer in their presence.

Resenting him for engendering those reactions in her, she replied tightly, "Trauma and reconstructive surgeon, yes."

Those eyes widened, those lips parted. Then both smiled and the world teetered. "This has to be fate," he drawled. "On more levels than one." Before she could make head or tail of this statement, his face turned grim, making her suspect she'd imagined the seconds-ago lightness. "There's been a pile-up on El-Eedan highway, Az-Zufranah's largest and, regretfully, most tempting for speeding, and the scene of the worst auto accidents in the last two years. Casualties in serious condition are estimated at sixty-four and rising. The first wave has already hit our ERs. In minutes they'll start sending patients to the ORs. We'll need all the help we can get. Think you're up to pitching in?"

It felt like a switch flipped inside her. Knowing that lives were in danger, that she was one of those who could help to save them, brought back the committed, resourceful, cool-under-fire person she'd been until a few minutes ago.

She straightened her shoulders, all enervation whooshing out of her body, determination and readiness flooding into its place. "Of course."

His gaze stilled on her for one of those slowed-down seconds, gauging the validity of her assurance. Then he nodded, his eyes giving no verdict away. "In that case, follow me."

She did, ran in his wake, seeing little besides him. Awareness of her surroundings finally intruded when they entered a scrubbing and gowning hall, the like of which she'd never seen. But, then, the whole complex was like nothing she'd ever seen. It felt as if it existed on some future earth where cost was no longer an issue and architecture and technology had leapt a century or two ahead and perfected the meld between esthetics, efficiency and decadent luxury.

"There's a women's hall, right through there."

She followed his pointing finger, wondering why there should be a separate women's hall, even in a country as conservative as Bidalya. Scrubbing and gowning was a unisex activity.

"Here's fine," she mumbled as she tried to catch her breath, stopped before a sink and picked up a scrubbing soap and brush.

Next moment both soap and brush went clattering into the stainless-steel sink. He'd turned his back on her and yanked his black sweatshirt over his head. He wore nothing underneath.

She snatched her eyes away, fumbled for the soap and began to scrub viciously. But it was too late. The sight of endless shoulders flowing into an acre-wide back, which in turn tapered down to a sparse waist, of steel muscles flexing and bulging under burnished skin the color of warm teak was burned into her retinas.

Now she understood why he'd recommended the women's hall. And *now* she remembered, though she hadn't worked with any, that there *were* surgeons who gowned over their underwear. Some not even that. She *wasn't* looking to see if he was one of those.

She should have followed his suggestion. She would next time.

She kept her eyes away. Not that it helped. She was still aware of his every move, his every breath as he came to stand facing her, thankfully across the five-foot partition separating the sinks. But he was so tall, six feet four or more, that she'd still get a good sight of those formidable shoulders if she looked up. She didn't. He was the one who was doing all the looking right now. She felt his eyes on her bent head and averted face, setting every inch they touched and examined on fire. She scrubbed harder.

It felt like they'd been caught in this time-distortion field for an hour when others came rushing in. The digital clock on the wall said it had only been two minutes. She recognized doctors and nurses, male and female. Two of the latter converged on him, helped him get gowned. A murmur had two more converge on her. In a minute they were gowned and she was running behind him again.

She followed him into a gigantic OR with eight stations for simultaneous surgeries. In the distance another door opened into a duplicate OR, then others after it and it felt like looking into facing mirrors reflecting images into infinity. That each OR was another high-tech setting intensified the impression. Many teams were already placing patients at each station.

Dr. Faress strode to a central position, shot out queries, in English. His people exchanged quick glances then each team answered in succession, in Arabic.

He extended a hand to her, making her move closer. "Dr. McPherson is our newest surgeon and until she picks up some Arabic, preferably not in an emergency setting, everyone will please speak English in her presence. Whether in the OR or outside it." A murmur of assent ran through the OR as he turned to her. "Now, let me translate. Main injuries are an evisceration, three closed abdominal injuries, three chest injuries and one pelvic fracture. All have compounding injuries, mainly extremity fractures. After aggressive resuscitation, on secondary survey they were all unstable, necessitating interruption of investigations and referral to us for surgical intervention."

She nodded, her eyes straying to the assortment of patients. “Do we have the latest vitals on each?”

Dr. Faress strode to the man who seemed to be organizing the transfer between ER and OR. Dr. Faress motioned to her as the man held up documents in succession because they couldn’t touch them. She moved closer, read the initial diagnoses and latest values. All the crash victims were in bad shape, but the worst one was the pelvic fracture case.

“Conscious all through,” Dr. Faress murmured. “No external injuries, no detection of intraperitoneal blood but he has a tense, distended abdomen and he’s in the worst hemodynamic condition.” He gazed down on her, as if asking her to solve this mystery.

It wasn’t one really. “They performed bedside FAST,” she said. “And it only detects free fluid in the chest and abdomen and misses retroperitoneal hemorrhage on a regular basis, even massive ones, which, with a pelvic fracture, he almost certainly has.”

Dr. Faress only nodded. And she knew that he’d already known that. So what had he been doing? Testing her?

He provided a nurse with the patient’s typing and cross-matching info, ordered fifteen units of blood then turned to her. "We'll deal with him first." He looked over his shoulder as he strode ahead. "Dr. Tarek, you're with us. Station 3."

She rushed beside him. "How about I take care of the evisceration case while you do that?" The woman displayed the second-worst set of vitals and rate of deterioration.

"Dr. Kamel will see to her. I want you with me."

He did? Why? To see for himself if she was really up to being a surgical trainer? That her expertise went beyond the theoretical? Did he think his establishment would have hired her if she didn't have enough credentials and experience? Any other time she would have, *might* have, succumbed to his testing. But putting his mind at rest wasn't a priority now.

She tried to point this out. "There's no need to have two surgeons working on the same patient, when each of us can lead a team handling a different patient."

He only gave her an unreadable glance, though his body language made his meaning unmistakable. *Please, proceed to the case I specified. Now.*

Chagrined, suppressing the overwhelming need to rush to another patient in danger, or shove him towards one, she gritted her teeth and hastened to precede him to the indicated station.

A first glance showed her that the patient's consciousness was now compromised, although resuscitation measures were top notch and hadn't been interrupted. Urgency rose within her as she and Dr. Faress rushed through a comprehensive but necessary exam.

After minutes of exchanging findings and conclusions in muttered trauma short form, her diagnosis was confirmed. If the hemorrhage wasn't stopped immediately, no resuscitation, no transfusion would make any difference. He'd keep bleeding out and die of hemorrhagic shock.

Dr. Faress's eyes found hers. "Your course of action?"

He *was* testing her. And being very blatant about it.

Without looking at him, she turned to Dr. Tarek, who'd turned out to be their anesthesiologist. "Conscious sedation, please. We'll go for embolization of bleeding arteries under angiography."

"You don't want a pelvic CT first?" Dr. Faress raised his hand in a wait-a-second gesture. "Or opt for surgical fracture fixation or hemorrhage control?"

"No unstable patient should be taken to the scanner, as I'm sure you know, Dr. Faress." She paid him the courtesy of answering in a tone low enough for his ears only. “Also, surgically fixing his pelvic fracture won’t stop his hemorrhage. And we both know open hemorrhage control mostly leads to death on the table.”

There. She hoped that was a good enough answer for him.

His eyes, those black on white hypnotic tools, narrowed. She wasn’t sure if it was with anger or amusement. Or was it appreciation?

A thrill passed through her when he corroborated her course of action to the anesthesiologist, hit a couple of buttons that brought an overhead angiographic machine whirring in place. He injected contrast material then they watched it bleeding in opaque clouds out of the injured arteries on the monitor.

He handed her an arterial catheter. “Go ahead.”

Without a second’s delay, she advanced the catheter to the first injury site, watching her progress on the monitor, then injected the material that would block the artery, sealing the injury.

It took twenty minutes to repeat the procedure in all injury sites. Finally, Dr. Faress injected more contrast material. It didn’t bleed out, showing that all arteries had been successfully sealed.

It was far from over, though. The patient had stabilized but there was still so much to do or the hard-won stability would only plunge into another spiral of deterioration.

Dr. Faress supported her opinion. "Now to the lesser dangers that can send us back to square one." Then she found out which reaction her earlier challenging answer had elicited when he gave her a melting smile and said, "Welcome to the team, Dr. McPherson. This patient is all yours."

With that, he gave her a slight nod and strode away.

She had a ridiculous urge to cry out for him to come back.

For God's sake! She'd gotten what she'd wanted, hadn't she? Recognition as a capable surgeon, and more patients treated simultaneously. *Then get to work, idiot.*

With a mental smack to her head, she plunged back into the place where she always went when she was operating on critical patients, forgetting all about herself until she pulled them out of danger.

It was two hours before she raised her eyes as her patient was wheeled away to IC, with another immediately replacing him. And she met Dr. Faress's eyes. He'd come back.

He didn't stay long. Only until he ascertained she'd made the right diagnosis with the current patient, took the right course of action. He helped her perform the trickiest part of the surgery then zoomed away to anther patient and another surgical team. And she realised what he was.

He was a maestro. He orchestrated what should have been chaos into a symphony of efficiency. He flitted between stations, dipping into each surgery at its most critical phase, performing that vital step that smoothed the path for her and the other surgeons to sail through the rest of the surgery without a hitch. It wasn't only her whose hand he chose to hold. He did it with everyone, with spectacular results. It was mind-boggling with some of the conditions that they lost no one. All thanks to him.

Sure, all the surgeons she worked with during the fifteen-hour struggle ranged from competent to superior, but in such a mass casualty situation, it took more than surgical skill to pull off something like saving every patient. It took multitasking leadership of a level she'd never witnessed, had never known existed.

Then the crisis was over, with all patients stabilized and in IC. And he'd disappeared. Thankfully.

With the exhilaration of an impossible feat accomplished seeping from her cells, exhaustion and the despondency that was now her natural state, and which had been lifted in the surreal time since she'd set eyes on Dr. Faress, settled back on her like a suffocating shroud. She stumbled out of OR, pondering life's latest cruelty.

As if she needed more upheavals she had to meet him. Not just a man who was a phenomenon in looks and effect, but one in efficiency, organizational and leadership skills as well as in surgical ones. She was certain he was someone all-powerful here, Head of Surgery at least. She'd probably end up exposed to each of his endowments on a regular basis. Her only hope was that her training project was something he had no interest in or no time for, that contact with him would be minimal or non-existent.

With her luck? Yeah. Sure.

She staggered out of the soiled room, the women's this time, found the restrooms, tried to regain a semblance of humanity before wandering out through the gigantic edifice.

She followed signs back to Reception, thinking she'd try to get back on the right track, hopefully permanently out of Dr. Faress's path. But with every step, just making her escape tonight became the only sane option.

Her steps were picking up speed when the distressing aromas of fresh-brewed coffee and fresh-baked pastries hit her. She swayed on her feet, moaned.

God. She was starving. It didn't help that her stomach was feeding on itself with tension. But she could wait one more hour…

A wave of dizziness put paid to that thought. She was no longer free to risk plummeting blood sugar levels. She owed it to her baby not to collapse.

Just as she turned in the direction of the aromas, another scent hit her. Even with OR overtones, it was unmistakably his.

It was her only warning before his touch on her arm followed, annihilating her balance. She stumbled, would have fallen, if not for him. Incredible speed and effortless strength took her fully against him as he steadied her back on her feet.

Gasping, her eyes tore to his face, found it inches away, the frank sensuality back in his eyes, his lips, drenching her in waves of imbalance and mortification.

"How will I beg your pardon for scaring you this way?"

She jerked away, tried to school her features, find her feet. "Y-you didn't… I'm just…tired and…and hungry, I guess…"

"Of course. You came expecting a sane first day

at work and got a fifteen-hour nightmare. But I promise you, it isn't always as merciless as that." His lips twitched. "Only every other day or so." She almost squeezed her eyes, felt her bones rattling with the blast of charisma. "Let me make it up to you." He extended a hand to her, command and courtesy made flesh and bone.

Her mind screamed for her not to take it, yet she gave him her hand as if it was his will that had control of it, not hers.

With her hand lost in his, she walked beside him in a daze to an elevator which looked straight out of a science fiction film set. It didn't feel as if it moved at all, but when the stainless-steel doors slid open it was onto a different landscape. A room the size of two tennis courts with a twenty-foot ceiling and floor-to-ceiling seamless windows spanning its arched side. They were *dozens* of floors up.

It was like looking out of a plane, with Az-Zufranah and its skyscrapers sprawling in the distance, lighting up the night sky like a network of blazing jewels. She dimly realized they must be in the glass-and-steel tower that soared heavenwards in the complex.

She'd barely recovered from the breathtaking sight and elevation when the opulence hit her, the exquisite taste, the sparseness of design and the power they conveyed. Then a huge desk with a state-of-the-art workstation at the space's far end hit her with the realization that this had to be his office.

He burnt another palmprint on her arm as he escorted her across a gleaming hardwood floor covered in acres of silk Persian carpets to a deepest burgundy leather couch ensemble with a unique Plexiglas and stainless-steel centerpiece table.

A tranquil gesture invited her to sit down. When she remained standing on legs she thought would never bend again, his hand gave her the gentlest of downward tugs, causing a widespread nervous and muscular malfunction. She collapsed where he indicated.

He stood before her, above her, towering, brooding, his eyes storming through her with that probing that made her feel exposed, vulnerable. Then his lips spread. Her heart tried its best to ram out of her throat.

"If you'll excuse me for a minute, I'll just order something to eat. Do you have any preferences? Any favorite cuisine?"

"Anything with calories," she croaked.

And he laughed. Her hand came up, pressing the spasm in her chest. He really shouldn't be allowed to do that. There should be a law against such potentially destructive behavior.

She snatched her eyes off him the moment he turned around, forced them downwards. They fell on a news magazine on the lower level of the table. He was on the cover.

It was clearly a picture he hadn't posed for, a close-up of him as he directed his medical forces during a crisis, much as he had during the past hours. His face was ablaze with concentration and determination, his authority burning up the page, imposing it on the most casual browsers, entrapping their wills and fascination.

The headline read: "HRH Sheikh Faress ben Qassem ben Hamad Aal Rusheed: Healer, Innovator, Peacemaker and Leader. Where will Bidalya's Renaissance Man Steer the Region?"

It took a full minute for the import of the words to register. Then realization detonated inside her mind.

He was the crown prince.

Realization crushed down on her with each passing second, each compounding implication. Until it hit bottom. She almost moaned out loud with the impact. *He was Jawad's brother.*

This was just too much. To meet him, of all people on her very first day in Bidalya. And not only to meet him, but to go to pieces at the sight of him, to all but drool over him. He was one of the two men she'd come to Bidalya to learn about.

Faress was the uncle of the baby she was carrying. Her dead sister's and his dead brother's baby.

CHAPTER TWO

FARESS'S lips twisted in self-deprecation.

He'd ordered "anything with calories", as Larissa put it. Literally. More food than ten people could eat in a whole day.

He had this hope that an excess of food might mitigate the craving to devour her.

He counted a dozen more defusing breaths before turning to his companion, only to have this hope vaporized. One glance and the heart that remained sedate through the worst crises zoomed, the breath that tightened only with brutal exertion was knocked out of him. Again. And she wasn't even looking at him this time.

His eyes dragged appreciatively over her, almost tasting the grace and femininity in her every line, his mind crowding with images of tasting it for real. His body tightened. Even more.

He shifted to relieve the pressure, shook his head in amazement. And to think he'd never gravitated towards Western women's beauty, contrary to most men of his culture. But it seemed that was because he hadn't seen *her*. Then he *had* and he'd known. *She* was the feminine ideal he'd never fully imagined, never thought existed, never thought he'd find, had now found.

He bit his lip on the rising hunger, forced voracious eyes up from the flare of hips which even her shapeless olive pants couldn't disguise, passed by the work-of-art hands clasped in her lap, those hands that wielded healing and not just the thrall that had shrouded him when she'd placed one in his. He bypassed breasts that even the loose shirt of her ensemble did little to hide their ripeness. It wasn't advisable to linger there, not now. But later…

He exhaled, swept up to the exquisiteness of her face, an oval of richest cream, a focus of vitality against the darkened hues surrounding her. It was framed by a heart-shaped hairline that flowed back into glossy tresses that now suffered the confinement of a severe ponytail. From his perspective, he could see it cascading its wavy locks down to her waist, a blaze of deepest, richest red that lit up the subdued ambiance he preferred.

He drew in another shuddering breath.

Bowled over. That was how he felt. Absolutely bowled over. And to think he'd pitied the flimsy characters who imagined such hyperbole, who reacted so ferociously to non-existent stimuli. He should have been careful with his disdain.

But he hadn't been. Thinking himself impervious to such frailties, he'd always been merciless in his judgement of people in the grips of thunderbolt attraction. And here he was, eating his every slashing statement and condescension. And loving it.

This Larissa McPherson must wield formidable magic. He'd never known such arousal at first sight. Or at all. Then he'd seen her standing at Reception and it had felt like he'd been hit by lightning that had left him at once powerless and super-powered.

It had been her eyes. Zapping him with her shock at the reaction he engendered in her, caressing him with her unconcealed wonder, gratifying him with her inability to look away. And it shouldn't have affected him this way. Women stared at him wherever he went, covetous, inviting, but their eyes and hunger on him had never thrummed self-satisfaction inside him, had mostly aroused annoyance, had rarely engendered reciprocating interest. When they did, it was a cerebral reaction. That of a connoisseur weighing up the pleasure value of what was on offer, and always finding it wanting. He'd never approached a woman, had only deigned to let those who pleased his eye enough and whom he deemed worthy the temporary distraction to do so.

Then there'd been her eyes. Those had engulfed him whole. And he hadn't only approached her, he'd barely stopped himself from pouncing on her before she dematerialized. But she hadn't.

Then he'd seen her eyes up close.

They were oceans that roiled with every heart-beat, changing hue with every thought that passed through her mind, every sensation that rippled through her body. They made him want to expose her to every stimulation there and then, so he could watch them flash through the spectrum of emotions, confessing all in spectacular, wordless color.

After her eyes had come her lips. Soft and small, flushed and plump. Parted, at a loss, reflecting his inability to apply brakes. He'd wanted them beneath his, to taste their every secret, suckle their every dimple, drain their every passion. He'd wanted them gasping in ecstasy, inviting his invasion, losing all inhibitions, clinging to his with a fever of their own.

Then she'd talked and he'd known what a siren's song sounded like. Then, as if all that hadn't been enough, she'd turned out to be a fellow surgeon. And a hell of a capable one.

She'd thrown herself headfirst into the tumult without batting an eyelid, had handled one surgery after another with all the versatility and level-headedness of a veteran surgeon, weathered the crashing waves of one extreme case after another when others had slunk away periodically for some much needed time out. She'd been the only one who'd kept up with his fifteen straight hours.

Then the woman of steel she'd become as soon as she'd donned her surgical gown had changed back into the creature of silk who'd captured his focus and sent his senses rioting, the moment no more endangered people had needed her strength and skills.

The switch was exhilarating, inflaming him with the need to witness yet another transformation, to the being of fire he knew she'd become at his touch, the one who'd match his ardor, until the conflagration consumed them both.

His gaze glided over features tailored to his every specific demand and set in a masterpiece of a bone structure, was drawn again to his foremost fascination, her eyes. Those eyes. He followed their downward gaze—and his heart contracted.

That magazine. What was it *doing* here?

With an inward groan he realized. Atef must have left it here in the hope Faress would succumb and read the unsanctioned if hugely flattering piece on him. His cousin still couldn't accept that Faress didn't share his pride over the international media's fascination with him, couldn't believe that he wasn't secretly excited about it, but was only resigned to it as part and parcel of being who he was. But while Faress had never sought or relished the attention, he hadn't exactly minded it either.

He did now. Her eyes were riveted to the damned cover.

So. She'd found out who he was. He was certain she hadn't known up till now. She hadn't recognized him on sight. Neither had she suspected his identity during the following hours. Not when he'd made it a royal decree to be addressed as Dr. Faress and never as *Somow'w'El Ameer* or Your Highness at work.

It was his reprieve from answering to the responsibilities of his inherited status, the only way to focus on those he'd chosen of his free will. It also stopped everyone from being too awed in his presence to function, created a semblance of ease in his working milieu. Not that it had been easy or was perfect. But when it had left her oblivious of his status today, he'd felt it had been worth every effort and discomfort. And now it was over.

He *had* known she'd find out sooner rather than later, but he'd hoped to remain only himself to her for a while longer. The man who'd sent awareness gushing in her system, arrhythmia into her heartbeat and imbalance into her limbs. The surgeon on whom she'd counted and with whom she'd fought alongside.

Now he'd cease to be that man and that surgeon to her and become the prince. He steeled himself against the calculation that would invade her expression, taint her body language as she estimated his net worth, the eagerness that no longer saw beyond his means and power, the coveting that had nothing to do with him and everything to do with what it meant to be coveted by him.

A breath of resignation burned out of his chest. He'd long been resigned to this, hadn't he? That along with privileges most men couldn't dream of, he forfeited what most men were *allowed* to dream of. Disinterested reactions and liaisons were foremost among those. At least he'd had her genuine interest for a few hours.

It had been nice while it had lasted.

But *no*. It hadn't been nice. It had been *glorious*.

Web'hagg'ej'jaheem...by *hell*, it should have lasted longer.

Didn't he deserve one solid day of sincerity in

his life? Couldn't Fate have waited until he'd gotten one kiss, one night meant for him, Faress the man, not Faress the prince?

A discreet buzz interrupted the rising tide of bitterness.

Larissa jumped at hearing it, as if at a nearby detonation.

Why was she so nervous? Worrying about what to do next? Trying to work out how to backpedal, how to fix what she must now be thinking had been her damaging behavior with him so far?

After those first minutes when he'd felt feminine greed lashing out of her like a solar flare, sending him hurtling towards her to get scorched, the crisis had occurred and she'd switched to her surgeon side, practical, composed, detached.

In that mode, she'd afforded him only the decorum a surgeon extended to a senior one, accepted his decrees only when she'd agreed with them. She'd offered him nothing beyond equality, with the implicit understanding she only did so as long as he reciprocated in kind. And *that* had been another unprecedented and truly magnificent experience. Would she start fawning over him now?

Ya Ullah. He wouldn't be able to bear it if she did.

That he'd look into her eyes and find the confession of equal attraction and the loss of control over it gone, replaced by artifice, by calculation, sickened him, infuriated him…

The buzz sounded again and his anger spiked as he realized what it was this time. Their food.

He stalked to the door, let in their food-bearers. Sensing his mood, they hastened in with the trolleys they'd brought then almost ran out, leaving him alone with her once more.

It turned out he'd ordered food enough for ten people for *two* days.

What the hell. She'd probably be even more impressed with his extravagance. He should just urge her to eat and get it over with. He now couldn't wait to send her away.

Before he could say anything she fumbled for a silver pitcher and a crystal glass, her hands shaking so much she splashed juice everywhere but inside her glass.

"Oh, God…" She set down her burdens with a clatter, lunged for paper napkins and started to dab at the spilled juice.

When she bent to dab at the carpet he growled, "Leave it."

His terse order brought her jackknifing up, her expression so complex many of its ingredients escaped his analysis. It contained exhaustion, which was only expected. There was also anxiety, befitting his expectations. But there was no trace of the false softening he'd dreaded, the cajoling deference. There was just the opposite, a tautening, a withdrawal. But it was something else he saw, felt but couldn't credit, that stunned him. Was that…dread?

She feared him?

A vise clutched his gut at the mere thought.

He strode towards her, anxious to dispel the suspicion, and her eyes shot up to him. The trepidation there was unmistakable.

"Larissa?" He cursed himself at the jolt of pleasure her name on his lips shot through him, now of all times. "You're not well?"

She jerked her eyes away as she shook her head. "I'm fine."

She *wasn't* fine. And, *b'Ellahi*, she *did* seem afraid.

Instead of her wanting to win his favor, his status caused her fear? The idea was insupportable.

"Larissa, are you afraid of me?" Her eyes widened at his abrupt question. "*B'Ellahi*—why? You think I brought you here to have you alone to—what? Accost you?"

Her eyes went round. It took her a full minute to blurt out, "God, *no*. How can you think that? It didn't even cross my mind."

"Are you sure?" he probed, hanging on her nuances, determined to test the veracity of her claim. "Or are you just saying that because you're afraid of my reaction if you said it did?"

She seemed at a loss for words again. Then she shook her head, exhaled on what sounded like incredulity. "Look, I can keep saying I'm not afraid of you and you can keep volleying back that I could only be saying that *because* I'm afraid of you until the cows come home. So once more, and hopefully for the last time. I'm *not* afraid of you. I don't even know where you got this idea."

He folded his arms over his chest, his lips twisting. "From the stricken expression on your face, that's where. I expect a lot of reactions when people learn I'm the crown prince but you were looking at this magazine as if it had just revealed to you that you were in the same room with Jack the Ripper."

For one terrible moment, as her lips, as her whole face trembled, he thought she'd burst out in tears.

She burst out laughing instead.

He stared at her, flabbergasted, almost wincing at her beauty as laughter overcame her, his heart kicking his ribs with each melodious peal. He'd never seen or heard anything so exquisite.

"Oh, God, excuse me," she gasped. "But you're just so far off base it's funny…" She tried to suppress her giggles, color creeping up her neck and face.

"I'm relieved you find my misreading of the situation so hilarious," he drawled, his voice heating with answering mirth, with relief, with his rising temperature. "Just what I was after."

Uncontrollable splutters escaped her containment efforts. "You're supplying comic as well as famine relief?"

He raised one eyebrow in exaggerated seriousness. "I pride myself on offering a comprehensive package to my co-workers."

And she spluttered again. Her chuckles drew out his own, even when each tinkle was tinged by the loss of control depletion wrought, twisting in his gut, tugging at his loins.

"And to put you *more* at ease, forget all about this crown-prince business. I consider myself a provisional one anyway."

That cut her laughter short, made her gape at him. "Huh?"

He didn't know why, but he needed to tell her this. "I have an older brother who's the rightful crown prince. But for reasons I won't go into now, he's left the kingdom. I prefer to think I'm warming the bench for him, as you Americans would say, and that he'll soon return and take back his rightful place."

She stared at him for another moment then wheezed again. "And that's supposed to put me at ease? Being only *second* in line to the throne of one of the most powerful oil states in the world is supposed to be less intimidating than being *first* in line?"

"Are you telling me you're intimidated?"

Her laughter spiked. "Hell, no."

He gazed at her, his heart expanding. *Ya Ullah*, she'd again pulverized his expectations. Nothing had changed. She still saw *him*, not the crown prince. His doubts had been unfounded. She was neither fawning nor intimidated. She was just being herself. Whatever chaos he'd thought he'd seen he must have imagined.

That meant he was free to resume the magic. To devour her.

And he would.

Larissa's hysterical laughter was aborted the moment Faress started prowling back to her, a predatory gleam in his eyes.

Every cell in her body surged in all-out alarm.

And she'd said she wasn't afraid of him?

She wasn't. Not that kind of fear. Not for a second.

Which might be very irrational, a scolding voice inside her tried to point out. He *was* all-powerful here, could literally get away with anything. And she was in his country, in his complex, in his den, in his absolute power. Maybe it was wise to be wary.

She wasn't. There was no doubt in her mind that he'd never harm anyone weaker than him, never abuse his power. While playboy was written all over him in phosphorescent foot-tall letters, protector was even more prominent. She'd been sure of that even before his anxiety when he'd thought her upheaval had been fear.

But upheaval was a mild word for what churned her guts into a tangled mess. And that was when shock still numbed her, when the predicament she'd stumbled into was still registering. She had no idea what it would feel like when it all hit bottom.

After being stunned by his misinterpretation she'd been enervated by the reprieve it had afforded her. Not that she could have blurted out the reason for her turmoil if it hadn't.

Yeah, *that* would have been priceless. *Oh, I'm not afraid of you, just afraid of losing my mind. I find myself falling at a man's feet for the first time in my life, find out he's all-powerful at my work, in my host kingdom—and the cherry on top? I'm carrying his older brother's baby. And by the way, the brother you hope will one day return and take his rightful place? He's dead!*

The situation was so untenable she'd almost lost control over the tenuous leash she'd had on the ever-simmering tears, her only outlet since Claire had died, so shockingly, just three weeks ago. In the struggle to withhold the weeping jags she'd been surrendering to ever since on a regular basis until she felt she'd dissolve, she'd started giggling like a demented hyena instead. She still felt the twitches of hysteria rippling beneath the surface of a fragile, artificial composure.

God, he'd spoken of Jawad with such longing. How could she leave him living in the futile hope of his return? How could she not? She couldn't reveal her secret now. The baby's safety and future were paramount. And she had no idea if those would be best served by having Faress and the Aal Rusheeds as his family.

He came to tower above her again, his eyes now steamy slits roasting her alive, almost scorching off the tethers of control.

"So this is your final verdict?" he drawled, his exotic accent deepening. "There's not now, and won't ever be, the least awe at me being the crown prince? You don't have the tiniest fear that I might abuse my power?"

"None," she rasped without hesitation.

And he smiled. That smile that should be banned under international law. "Good." And that should be, too. That satisfied lion's rumble. "Now I will say and do anything, everything, without worrying about your interpretation."

"My interpretation?"

"That you won't fear yourself in any danger if you react as you please to my advances."

"Advances?"

He leaned down, a lazy hand reaching behind her, extracting her ponytail, bringing it thudding over her breast. It hit her nipple through the thickness of her shirt, sending a hail of stimulation to her core. She jerked, almost moaned.

She couldn't believe, let alone understand, what he was doing to her. He hadn't touched her beyond a courteous touch on her arm or hand, he'd done nothing but expose her to his sight and sound and scent, and he was teaching her what it meant, what it felt like to be at her senses' mercy. To know that they had none.

He straightened, taking a long lock with him, winding it round and round his surgeon's fingers.

Then he finally drawled, a mouth-watering smile drenching his fathomless baritone, "Do you hear an echo, or is it just me?"

She did hear ringing in her ears. He was teasing her, was coming on to her…She grimaced at the inappropriate, flimsy description. He certainly wouldn't do anything as pathetic and cheap as coming on. He'd put his intentions far better, far clearer. He was *advancing*. Like an unstoppable conquering army.

He suddenly came down beside her with a movement of such economy and grace it should have been impossible for someone of his height and bulk. Her heartbeats piled up like the vehicles had in that catastrophe they'd just finished dealing with.

He gave her a smoldering sideways glance, noting her condition with satisfied eyes. "Hmm, the echo seems to be gone." He picked up the silver pitcher, poured a glassful of pineapple juice. "This was what you were attempting a few minutes ago, wasn't it?" She stared at him mutely as he brought the glass to her lips. "Drink, Larissa. Drought relief. Part of the comprehensive service."

She didn't know how she did it, but she downed the whole thing in what felt like one gulp. He was too close, he'd emptied her lungs of air, her mind of reason. His next words emptied the world of both.

"You will come stay at my place."

The words sank, exploded like depth mines in her mind.

Shock surged to the surface in their wake, "*your place*" almost exploding out of her. She barely caught back the echoing words, croaked instead, "Uh—thanks—I—I already have an—an apartment, in Burj Al Taj…and—and it's spectacular…"

"I don't doubt the level of luxury of whatever accommodation the project provided. That's not the issue. I want you with me." She only stared at him, too dumbstruck to even formulate a reply, flabbergasted at the speed with which everything was happening, at his sweeping advances through her barriers. His lips tilted again. "You don't have to be *with* me, if it's too soon for you. You can be at one of my guest houses in my palace's grounds and be as far as a few blocks away. If it isn't too soon, don't use irrelevant inhibitions to talk yourself out of it."

"For God's sake, we just met today!" she spluttered.

His shrug was dismissal itself. "What is time when the first minutes tell you more about someone than years do about others? When in hours we shared what most people live whole lives together without sharing? Look beyond the restrictions of custom and the expected, Larissa. Look at the reality of us, me and you, man and woman. Nothing else matters."

He'd missed his calling, being a surgeon. He should have been a hypnotist. A sorcerer. Then again, he was probably both.

When she kept gaping at him, he sighed, sat forward, dragged one trolley closer, arranged a few plates and bowls of the most incredible, hand-painted china she'd ever seen in front of her.

He spread a deep red silk napkin on her lap then spooned something with a browned surface and creamy depths and brought it to her lips. She opened them without volition, felt warm, rich sweetness the consistency of thickest cream melting over her tongue, contrasting with the chewiness of the caramelized crust and the coolness of the silver spoon. She moaned at the sheer decadence, the brutal seduction of the whole experience.

"You like it, hmm?" He wanted her to verbalize it? Not satisfied with seeing her almost fainting with liking it all? The food, what he was doing to her…*especially* what he was doing to her? He gave her a glance of all-male satisfaction, admiring his handiwork, added another touch, wiping a lazy finger over a smudge on her upper lip. "*M'halabeya* is made of milk and cream and honey and ground rice. Every food group you need to replenish you now."

Her stomach wailed, loudly, for another taste. Another touch. With indulgence filling his eyes and lips, he fed her the whole bowl, eliciting almost non-stop uncontrollable murmurs of appreciation, at the care and seduction in his every move as the much-needed sustenance hit her bloodstream.

He finally drew back, his eyes heavy with so much she didn't dare name. Then he advanced again, his face nearing hers in agonizing slowness, sending all her hairs standing on end. An inch away, he parted his lips, let a gust of intoxicating breath singe her cheek before he closed his lips over the corner of her mouth. Just as the dim lights started to go out completely, he opened his lips again, swept the tip of his tongue in a warm, moist caress, licking at what must have been a smear of *m'halabeya*.

She jerked as if with an electrocuting current. It seemed this jolted something undone inside him, too. He drew away, one hand cupping her head, the other tilting her chin backward. Then he waited, his obsidian gaze tattooing her retinas.

She knew what he was asking, what he'd do if

she didn't say no as her mind was screaming for her to. She had to breathe first to produce sound. And she couldn't breathe.

Growling something dark in his chest, his head descended, his lips besieging hers, detonating more depth mines in her blood. He didn't open his lips over hers, didn't breach their paralyzed seal with his tongue, just kept nuzzling her like an affectionate lion.

The he finally took his lips away an inch, groaned, as if in pain, "Kiss me, Larissa. Take what you need of me, *ya jameelati*."

"Is—is that an order?" she hiccuped, stunned that her speech center wasn't fried. "As my superior? Or as the crown prince?"

He let her go at once. She fell back in a heap on the couch.

He sat for a long minute, affront radiating from him. Then he exhaled, leaned a forearm on one formidable thigh. "Outside work, there'll never be orders between us. *If* they're not part of intimate games, that is. I wouldn't even approach you if you didn't want me as much as I want you. As we both know you do."

She wasn't even going to contest that. That would be the height of hypocrisy and coyness. Two things she wasn't equipped with. They both *did* know.

But it was impossible. On every sane and ethical basis, she had to put an end to this. Right now. She inhaled deeply.

"Listen, Dr. Faress—er…Your Highness—"

"Faress," he interrupted, terse, uncompromising. "No titles when you're addressing me, and certainly never, *ever* Your Highness. I call you by your name, you call me by mine. Now say it. I need to hear my name on your lips."

"All right. *Faress…*" She faltered, shocked at the jolt of pleasure saying his name shot through her. "It goes without saying you're used to women throwing themselves at your feet. And though I can certainly see the attraction, can't pretend not to feel it, what matters is if I act on it, and I'm not going to. Not now, not ever. This morning, right now, you just keep taking me by surprise. I never had any experience with anyone so—so potent that I just keep freezing, keep being swept along. But no matter what I want, the bottom line is I'm not here to fool around with some over-endowed, over-powerful, over-privileged crown prince!"

Silence clanged in the wake of her summation. He'd gone still, his face a heart-rendingly beautiful and unreadable mask.

Oh, God. She'd pushed her luck too far. Now he'd be angry. He might even send her packing if he believed he wouldn't have his way with her. Which, for every reason there was, he wouldn't.

After a nerve-racking moment, he threw his awesome head back and laughed. And laughed.

He finally brought himself under control, chuckles still rumbling in his chest like distant thunder. "*Ya Ullah*…I don't know which is more gratifying. Feeling you coming undone at my touch, knowing every tremor passing through you is fueled by genuine hunger, or hearing your denunciation and knowing that every word passing through your lips is fueled by genuine conviction."

So he believed she meant her rejection. Good. *She* wasn't sure she did. Which was just too infuriating. She was here to see if he was guardian material for their dead siblings' baby, not fling material. Which was no doubt what he had in mind. A very short fling. Probably a one-night stand. But at least, and unbelievably, he didn't seem to mind her rejection. She'd thought someone with his power, no matter what he professed, would be offended if even such a fleeting offer of his was turned down.

"And of course I don't mind." He'd read her mind! "I said I expect you to be totally free in your reactions to my advances. My word is considered law in most circumstances, and the first one to abide by it is myself. But advances aside, you will come and stay at my place, for as long as you're here in Bidalya."

That long? "But I already refused…" she faltered.

"You refused involvement. And while I concede your right to more time, I'm demanding that you stay at my place. Anything more is at your pace."

She opened her mouth in an unformulated protest and he raised an imperious hand. "I insist. I don't know how a female doctor ended up alone at the other end of the city. There's going to be hell to pay for this serious lapse."

She found words then. "If that's your concern, you can offer me something near the complex with one or more other females."

"I can, but I won't. In my place you share my invisible protection and I have peace of mind about your safety."

"You make it sound as if Bidalya is a very dangerous place for a single woman."

"A beautiful woman living alone, even in societies where this situation has become a fact of life, is still subject to varying levels of dangers. One of your caliber of beauty here can and will draw all sorts of unsavory attention."

"For God's sake, your women are the beautiful

ones!" she exclaimed. "No one's going to give me a second glance."

"You mean like I didn't?" OK, he had a point there. *Not* that she could understand why he was giving her that attention. He went on, "And, then, our women never live alone and our men are used to their brand of beauty. You, on the other hand..." He paused, pursed his lips. "I'm not even going into the possibilities."

"You offer all foreign female doctors the same protection?"

"They're set up together in hotels and assigned guards, or live in secured compounds. Outside their residence they're told that if they breach the safety instructions we impose, they breach their contracts. You, I want with me."

OK. That was succinct. *Whoa.*

"So all you're offering me is a place to stay?" she rasped. "You don't expect anything in return?"

His smile grew bone-liquefying. "I expect everything. But not in return for anything. Ever. Only when you can't bear not giving it to me. And then all I'm offering that you can't obtain on your own is absolute security. You insisted you don't fear me." He paused. "Though here you need more than that, you need to trust me."

"I *do*."

At the swiftness, the certainty of her admission, his black eyes blazed. "You honor me."

Yeah. And you stagger me, she almost blurted out in return.

She didn't, probably because a question was overriding all her thought processes. She asked it. "But I can still say no? I can opt for what you offer every other female doctor?"

"You can say anything you like," he said. "But you won't." He cupped her cheek, aborting what would have been a vigorous nod of assent. "And though you can stay at a distance, that isn't where I'll stay. I plan on wallowing in this incredible thing we have."

She almost choked on her lungs. "We don't have anything…"

"We do. And it's undeniable, unstoppable." He leaned to brush his firm, cool lips against the scorched skin at her jaw before pulling back. "And I won't be either denied or stopped. But as I said, we'll go at your pace. My patience is legendary. Now, let's stock you up with more calories."

And for the next hour he fed her things she'd never tasted before, delicacies of his land, shared every bite with her as he told her their names and how they were made.

She surrendered to his ministrations, the urge

mounting to tell him that if the baby she carried wasn't all that mattered, if her obligation to give him the best possible future by making clear, rational choices, Faress might not have needed to be patient at all.

But as it was, no amount of patience would do him any good. No matter how much she longed to, she wouldn't, *couldn't*, succumb to his annihilating temptation.

Faress didn't know how long it had been as he indulged in that most erotic experience of his life, feeding Larissa, sharing every bite with her. All he knew was that with the need for food totally sated, other hungers reigned, threatening to overwhelm his restraint. It was time to put some distance between them. Before he damned to hell all resolutions to savor this, to give her time, and seduced her here and now.

He put the fork down, cupped her velvet cheek in his large palm, feeling as if he was filling it with rose petals. He almost groaned with the surge of arousal. "Say yes, Larissa."

Another surge of color answered him before she nodded, averted her eyes. And he'd bragged about his patience?

He rose on legs stiff with leashed hunger, stalked

to his desk to arrange her stay, trying not to look back at her every other step. He failed. Her effect on him was deepening.

Added to all she was, her resistance, another precedent, only made his eagerness for her mount by the second.

Ya Ullah, so this was how a bull felt with a red flag waved in front of it!

The challenge, the taunt of her indignant rejection had been almost too much to resist. He'd almost charged at her then and there, pulverized her resistance, as he had no doubt he could, would, if he wanted to. And how he wanted to.

But he hadn't. He wouldn't. He'd wait. He'd delay his gratification. She was worth every ache and frustration. There was no doubt in his mind she was the lover who'd been made to unleash his abandon, open up the endless promise of intimacy and pleasure.

She'd be the exception. He'd court her, for as long as it took. And he had every opportunity to do so with her working side by side with him, staying near, day and night, so close yet so far, heightening the torment, honing the craving. He'd wallow in her resistance as he wore it down. And when it finally crumbled…

He hit a button, grappling with his impatience

for the conflagration when it did, groaned as anticipation wrenched through him. This was going to be unrepeatable.

CHAPTER THREE

LARISSA leaned her head against the upholstered side of Faress's opulent limousine, her eyes wide, gazing at the splendor of Az-Zufranah at night as it rushed by. And taking in none of it.

She could barely breathe with him so near, could feel nothing but his aura, his scent inundating her. Even though he was across the expansive eight-foot back seat, she felt as if he was touching her all over. Which he was, with his gaze.

God, he was so imposing. Everything he'd said and done had been arrogant, overriding and, if she had the mental stamina to deal with anger, infuriating. Or at least it would have been from anyone lesser. Anyone else. But from him, a superior creature in every way, one who oozed entitlement and radiated personal power and charisma, everything he'd said and done had felt so—so *right*. She'd found it exhilarating, captivating, overwhelming.

Which wasn't why she was doing this! She'd

succumbed to his invitation, rather this decree, for a good reason. The best.

A voice inside her insisted again she was just emotionally exhausted, that she'd just done so because it was a blessed relief not to have to make decisions, have someone else take charge, give her a break. She smothered that voice yet again.

This opportunity he'd offered her was something she couldn't have dreamed of before coming here. Since she'd discovered that Jawad, the brother-in-law she'd worshipped and who'd died just a week before Claire had, hadn't been the orphan he'd claimed to be, but had instead been the heir to the throne of Bidalya, that she wasn't the only family the baby she was carrying for him and Claire had left, she'd been feverishly projecting the possibilities. That *was* the family Jawad had renounced, and she'd heard Bidalya's king wasn't considered a benevolent one. She owed the baby a family, but certainly not if they were a family of dictators.

When she'd found out about Bidalya hosting a unique opportunity for GAO volunteers, sponsoring their training in its state-of-the-art hospitals, she'd thought it the perfect opportunity to enter Bidalya. She'd signed up for a three-month stint as a trainer in her field and had been accepted on the spot. All she'd hoped for then had been second-hand knowledge through distant observation. It had certainly never occurred to her that she'd meet Faress on her first day here.

But she had, and he was offering her an up-close-and-personal chance to find out about him and about his family, people from a different culture, and royalty to boot, whom she knew nothing about as a people, let alone as individuals.

She *was* right to grab at the chance. What better way to gain the measure of the baby's uncle than be in his private milieu, where she was sure the real man would reveal himself?

She couldn't even presume to know anything about him yet. He was incredibly efficient as a surgeon, authoritative as a man, irresistible as a male. But that made him neither a despot nor suitable guardian material. There was far more she needed to know before she risked taking a step further.

As another voice told her it would have been enough to gauge his character at work, she silenced it saying that getting to know him in professional situations wouldn't have helped her gauge how he'd react in deeply and distressingly personal circumstances.

No. It was the best idea to be at his “place”, as he’d put it. It was the right thing to do.

Suddenly he reached out, took her hand in his and tugged, bringing her half against him, where she remained in an enervated heap for the rest of what seemed like an endless drive. And she no longer knew up from down, right from wrong.

“You didn’t tell me I’d be rooming with Scheherazade.”

Faress gazed down at Larissa and thought this was what fire would be like made flesh, made woman.

Her hair flamed its richness in the flickering light of a dozen strategically placed oil lamps. Her lips, deepened to crimson, scorched him with promise. The rest of her, her spirit, her wit, her passion, blazed even brighter.

He smiled at her quip. After oohing and aahing over the exterior of the palace-annexed buildings with their ancient architecture, he’d felt she’d been let down by the lesser authenticity of the interiors. She’d lapsed into silence until they’d entered the guest house where she would stay. Just as he’d thought it was depletion silencing her, her eyes, exhausted as they were, had flared with pleasure.

He’d just known she’d appreciate this place. It was his favorite among all the guest houses, the one whose construction, decoration and furnishing he'd personally overseen. He'd wanted it as a special place for his special guests.

The strange thing was, since its completion, he hadn't considered anyone special enough to bring here. Now he had.

Maybe he *had* constructed this place for her.

He now watched her running a hand over the back of an Egyptian mosaic, hand-carved chair, her lips spreading at what he knew was its perfect smoothness, before she turned her attention to a spherical, glass and burnished brass lantern hanging from the ceiling with long, spectacular brass chains. The hypnotic play of light and shadows it created cascaded over her, adding an unearthly effect to her beauty, deepening her magic.

He shook his head at his ebbing control.

Then she turned to him with a smile that almost had him plunge them here and now in what he knew they were destined to drown in sooner or later.

Oblivious to his state, she picked up a handwoven silk brocade pillow off an *areekah*, a low couch upholstered in matching fabric, ran her fingers over the delicate patterns, still smiling at him. "This place is beyond belief. It feels like a trip back in time all rolled in one with a visit to the future."

He couldn't return her smile. He ached too much. "I didn't think anyone would appreciate a literal plunge into the times of 'One Thousand and One Nights', hence the ultra-modern amenities."

"You thought right. It's amazing to walk through doors that look like they've been transported through millennia intact, only for them to swing open soundlessly with a voice recognition and fingerprint sensor. I'm sure even Scheherazade's imagination couldn't have come up with anything like this place."

He attempted a smile when all he wanted was to devour hers off her lips. "I'm sorry the authenticity doesn't extend to providing her as a roommate. But since she's not here, do you think you can stand in for her?"

"Why? Are you standing in for Scheherayar?"

"I hope I don't have anything in common with an insecure loon who had to be defused for almost three years by tales any four-year-old would have recognized as purest fantasy in a minute."

She chuckled. "I take it you despise the guy, huh?"

He raised both eyebrows. "The character who did

more than the region's historical despots and madmen combined to give men around here an indelibly bad reputation? What makes you think that?"

She chuckled again. "Now that you put it so eloquently, nothing at all. So how can I stand in for Scheherazade if you're not into fairy tales? Not that I know any worth telling."

"I want you to tell me a real story. Your story."

It was as if he'd just told her he wanted her to jump into a pit full of scorpions.

She lowered her eyes as she put down the pillow, yanking away the expression of absolute panic from his alarmed scrutiny. Next second she raised her eyes again and it was gone.

Ya Ullah, was he so afraid anything would ruin the perfection that he kept imagining non-existent reactions in those eyes to torment himself with?

"It's three a.m., Faress…" She hesitated over his name, the second syllable wobbling. He barely bit back the demand for her to say it again, confidently, intimately. "I don't think it's time to recount my life story."

He stared at her, unable to believe he'd been so insensitive.

He groaned. "*Aassef*—sorry for such an untimely demand. I completely lost track of time, which is your doing, of course. But this makes it twenty hours since we first met…" And it felt like it had been twenty days, weeks even. "And you've been through hell for fifteen of them, and that right after flying across the world only the day before. It's a marvel you haven't collapsed yet."

He walked to her, bent and touched his lips to her cheek, withdrew in time to see those eyes going a scalding shade of violet. It was such a bitter-sweet ache, this holding back. He'd never denied himself a woman he wanted. But, then, there'd never been anyone he'd wanted enough that he'd felt he'd been denying himself letting her go. He'd certainly never imagined feeling deprivation gnawing at him. As it was now.

And it was glorious. And maddening. And he'd better end his exposure to her before he dragged her to the floor and feasted on her.

He straightened, trying to ease the heavy throb clamping his body from the neck down. "Now I'll reprogram the door mechanism to your voice and fingerprint, teach you how to time the lock to open for the housekeepers and caterers I assigned to you when you're not around. Take tomorrow off. Or as much time as you need."

She raised her shoulders, let them drop in depletion. "If I hit the shower then bed in thirty minutes, I'll be at work at eight a.m. sharp. I just finished one of the most grueling residency programs in the States where I learned that sleep is an over-rated luxury as well as something I can function at optimum without."

He scowled. "Take tomorrow off. That is an order."

"I thought you said there won't be orders except in…er…"

"Intimate games?" he drawled, imagining those games, groaning at their vividness, their effect, when she spluttered to a halt. "None as yet, *ya jameelati*. This is work-related. Get reacquainted with the concept of sleep. That's a direct order from your boss."

Her eyes became round. "You're my…?"

"Boss? You didn't know that?"

"N-no. I thought you were Head of Surgery at least, but I didn't think you'd be directly involved in the project. Actually, I was hoping you—"

"Wouldn't be?" He finished for her when her words dribbled into silence. "So you wouldn't see much of me? You hope I won't make time for you after all? Or that work will be regular eighteen-hour days and you'll be here only to crash?"

He could see his rationalizations were accurate from the mortification staining her expression. Disappointment spread like ice down his spine until she said, "That was before…before…"

"Before you got to know me a bit?" She nodded her assent. He inhaled. "I was that horrible during the crisis you wished not to see me again?"

"No, *no*." She brought both hands to her head. "Oh, please, quit interrogating me. I don't know anything any more, OK?"

He groaned again. "*Aassef marrah tanyeh, ya* Larissa. Sorry once again for testing the limits of your endurance. Let's get you acquainted with the workings of your place, then I *will* leave you to sleep this time."

He extended a hand to her, was relieved when after a moment's hesitation she put hers there, all soft and pliable, let him guide her through the guest house. She was a quick study, getting the hang of the complex mechanisms running the place in minutes.

The last thing was the door, and after they'd re-programmed it, she murmured and touched it open.

He stepped across the threshold, her hand still in his. He lifted it to his lips, pressed a kiss into her palm. He felt the shock wave that his touch sent through her, and the equal response it detonated inside him.

"Tomorrow you will take off, Larissa," he murmured. "Show up at work and I'll only haul you back here."

Then before he hauled her into his arms and to bed, he forced himself to turn and walk away.

Larissa watched Faress prowling away along the ingeniously landscaped pathway, tried to tear her eyes off him.

Even with his back to her, she was swooning at the sight, the very idea of him. She'd surely done her level best to feed what must be the planet-sized ego of a playboy of unimaginable scope.

She couldn't fool herself it had been her steadfastness that had sent him to his palace now. And he knew it, had once again made certain of his irresistibility. That he'd chosen to walk away had been no thanks to her. It seemed he was satisfied with the completion of phase one in his plan for her. Whatever that was.

And why should she even pretend to puzzle over that? His plan was clear. He wanted to add her to his acquisitions. Which still dumbfounded her. He was no doubt a connoisseur of women, took his pick of the world's most perfect beauties, and that he'd decided he wanted her on sight was unbelievable…

What was more unbelievable was that she was flattered out of her mind, was fluttering so hard at the idea of his desire she was shaking all over. He had played her like the virtuoso he was, and she'd all but melted in his hands. She should resent him for that alone, for the siege he'd laid to her, the pre-emptive strikes he'd hit her with, one after another.

But no matter how she tried to resist him, to shake off his hypnotic effect, it was still a struggle not to run after him and blurt out the truth of who she was and why she was here.

Only his effect on her held her back. It made everything she was thinking and feeling unreliable. And with her reason shot to hell, she couldn't take any step now when she'd probably be committing an irretrievable mistake.

After all, a man like him—if men like him existed—lord of all he surveyed from birth, a man used to having people bow down to his every whim…what would he do if she told him the real reasons she was in Bidalya?

Her revelations would be a brutal blow on so many levels. A deep personal loss at Jawad's death and a huge responsibility, maybe even a threat from Jawad's unborn child's existence. She had no idea what it would mean to the kingdom's stability to introduce a male child of an estranged crown prince, a new heir to the throne. There was no telling what Faress would do in response.

What if he accused her of lying? What if, in his

fury, he shed all the refinement she'd experienced so far? What if he detained her until he'd made sure of her claims? And when he did, what if his reaction and subsequent actions were extreme?

Despite his overwhelming charm, his finesse as a man and superiority as a surgeon, she sensed there was ruthlessness in him, the stamp of his royal Middle Eastern blood. She did trust him when it came to treating women, to never imposing himself where he wasn't wanted. But in extreme situations, what would a prince, on whom a whole country depended to keep order and peace, consider ethical? Ethics, morality, even basic right and wrong might be different for him than for the rest of lesser mortals.

Then came the wild card of his blatant interest in her and her reciprocating, helpless attraction to complicate everything. Instead of this being a factor to secure her a favorable reaction, gain her leniency in case of an unfavorable one, she believed it would be what turned this situation into a volatile mess. The plunge from potential mistress material into potential major trouble-maker was far steeper that if she'd been a female he'd had no interest in. He'd probably be more ruthless with her on account of the thwarted expectations or the humiliation factors alone.

No. She couldn't tell him about her pregnancy. Not now. Now more than ever, she needed to stick with her original plan. She'd gather information, decide whether to tell him and his family of the baby's existence or go home without telling them and raise the child alone.

That was the thing to do. She knew it… So why were a dozen voices inside her telling her she was doing everything wrong?

Oh, God, the only truth she'd told him had been when she'd told him she didn't know anything any more.

Enough. There was one way she could think of to handle this.

Until she could tell up from down again, had found out more about him and could predict his reactions with any semblance of objectivity, she was keeping her secrets.

She took the day off. Or rather the day took *her* off.

She blinked at the digital clock on her bedside table proclaiming the time six a.m. The next day. She'd slept twenty-four hours straight. She hadn't even roused from her sleep to visit the bathroom.

Not that it should surprise her. Grief had already compromised her stamina. It was only because of the baby that she hadn't allowed it to overcome her. Now add shock, jet-lag, exhaustion, early pregnancy, the most devastating encounter of her life and the expectation of far more upheaval to come, and she should be grateful she hadn't gone catatonic.

She lay in bed, still disoriented, wondering that her eyes weren't swollen, that it had been the first time she hadn't wept herself to sleep since Claire's death, staring at the soaring, domed, whitewashed ceiling of this incredible bedroom.

Just like the rest of the guest house, it was enormous, painted in warm earth colors and furnished with the most exquisite, hand-carved and painted Middle Eastern furniture. Only the soothing light of a corner brass lantern, this time decorated with stained glass in the famous Arabian windows design, lit the room. Daylight couldn't breach the seal of the blackout curtains.

She placed a languid hand over her lower abdomen. It was too soon to feel anything. At seven weeks, there was no external evidence of her pregnancy. Yet it had changed her whole life. More, it now ruled her life. And now there was Faress…

She sprang up in bed, tearing the hand-embroidered Egyptian cotton bedspread off her suddenly steaming body.

What was Faress doing in the same thought that dwelt on what ruled her life?

She leaned forward, dropped her head in her hands.

The numbness of shock, the surrealism that had cloaked her time with Faress was evaporating. It left her feeling exposed, vulnerable. She'd never felt that way before. Not even when she'd lost Claire, her sister, her lifetime companion and best friend.

And you can stop feeling this way.

Exhaling forcibly, she rubbed her face, sprang out of bed. She'd better shower and dress. And head to work. Some action should jog her back to normal.

In an hour she was ready, her step determined as she crossed the guest house. Until her eyes fell on her reflection in the ornate full-length, mother-of-pearl-inlaid mirror at the end of the hall and her steps faltered. She groaned.

She'd dressed in a less shapeless ensemble, in a more vivid green, one of the most flattering colors for her complexion. Worse, she'd left her hair loose and it was now cascading in undulations down to her waist. Worst of all, she'd done all that unconsciously. Any guesses why?

Tossing a glance at the wall clock, she groaned again.

There was no time to change. She had no idea how she'd get to work yet, or how far the palace was from the complex. She couldn't even estimate the time the trip had taken when Faress had brought her here. Her senses had been distorted by his nearness.

She exhaled, reached into her handbag, got out a ponytail holder, swept her hair back and imprisoned it. At least she now didn't look like some wild woman.

Squaring her shoulders, she stalked to the door, activated the voice and touch sensors. The door slid open. Next second she almost slid in a heap to the floor.

Faress was approaching from the far end of the corridor of foliage and flowers, clad in casual whites and beiges, the understated elegance and light colors making him look bigger, more perfect than she remembered.

She watched with a thundering heart as he undulated towards her like a lazy lion, primal poetry permeating his every move, the seven a.m. Bidalyan sun striking dark blue highlights on his raven mane and a golden glow off his bronzed skin.

And she'd been telling herself she'd exaggerated his impact. She'd actually done a great job of diminishing it in her memory, in the hope of reducing it to manageable proportions, no doubt.

His face remained unsmiling all the way, his mood totally unreadable with his uncanny eyes and the amazing spectrum of emotions they were capable of displaying hidden behind mirrored sunglasses. But she could feel his focus like a laser beam frying her heat-regulating center, sending her temperature soaring.

He kept coming, didn't seem he'd stop, would bump into her. She stood her ground. More out of having no volition rather than any resolve to defy his power over her. And he didn't stop.

He didn't bump into her either. He embraced her instead, the loosest of embraces, what could have been, from anyone else, the most casual of greetings. From him, it felt as he'd surrounded her, invaded her, absorbed her.

Then too late, too soon, he drew away.

"Sabah'l khair, ya jameelati." His husky whisper drenched her, his scent, the amalgam of freshness, Arabian musk and his own maleness making her dizzy with every breath she snatched. "That's good morning, my beauty. Word for word. Make note of them. Time to get you down to some Arabic basics."

Another wave of heat swept through her. "I doubt I'll ever find use for or a chance to say, '*Ya jameelati*,'" she breathed.

"But now you'll know what I'm calling you, *ya helweti*. That's my sweet." He took her hand to his lips, marked her knuckles one at a time in feathery kisses. "Had a good day's sleep?"

She winced. "You're rubbing my nose in that 'I can function at optimum without sleep' statement, aren't you?"

"You think I'd indulge in I-told-you-sos?"

She stared up at him. It was an impossibility to imagine him indulging in any pettiness of any sort, even in jest. And she'd implied he would, even if in part-mortification, part self-deprecation. The problem was, from his tone, his expression, she had no idea if he was affronted or amused.

"Uh—I'm sorry. I…" she started.

His hand came up, his forefinger touching her lips. The feeling of his firm, warm flesh touching hers struck her mute.

"I'm not," he murmured. "I love the way you don't watch what you say around me. I want you to promise me you never will."

Distress coughed out of her. "I won't promise it, I guarantee it. If you'd asked that I should, we would have had a problem."

He took off his sunglasses and his eyes flashed. She almost squeezed her eyes shut at the intensity in his. That lasted one more second before it dissolved into teasing. "Does your guarantee include saying what comes to your mind, whenever it comes, unadorned?"

"I may not be able to hold reactions back, opinions, but as for other thoughts…"

"You mean you'd be embarrassed to voice those?" When his probing was met by her suddenly finding her shoes very interesting, a gentle finger coaxed her gaze back to him. "We'll discuss why later. For now I'll be satisfied with how well rested you look. I'm glad you rediscovered the benefits of sleep."

She nodded, relieved he'd changed the distressing subject. "Did I ever. My batteries are overcharged and I'm raring to go to work. So if you'll just let me know how to get there…"

He gave her a look of mock surprise. "You mean you haven't guessed my real motive for having you near? That it's all a ploy so we'd commute to and from work together and save fuel?"

She stared at him, elation bursting inside her. He intended to escort her to and from work on a regular basis!

Struggling to suppress her reaction, berating herself for its stupidity, its inappropriateness, she attempted a wavering smile. "Since you of all people can't be worried about fuel consumption I assume you're being environmentally conscious."

"Of course. So—are you ready?"

On the surface it sounded as if he meant ready to go to work. But she knew he meant ready for him and more of his advances.

Knowing she should say no, ask him for a separate transport, or insist she'd arrange her own, she nodded mutely.

He didn't even blink in reaction. Waiting for verbal consent?

She gave it to him. A hitching, tremulous, "I'm ready."

That was another mistake, but right now she felt anything was worth the warmth that kindled his obsidian eyes.

He took her elbow in a possessive large palm, making her feel protected, coveted, steered her along the seclusion of the wide, long pathway into the open landscape of the palace's grounds.

With every step beside him, every breath that breathed him in, his virility, his uniqueness, she berated herself for breaking her promise to him so soon, so totally.

Telling him she was ready wasn't only embellishing what she said in his presence, it was an outright lie.

CHAPTER FOUR

'I WOULD be lying if I said I didn't think I'd bitten off more than I could chew, organizing this project," Faress said as he poured Larissa an Arabian cardamom coffee before taking another bite of *khobez*, the unleavened, incredibly tasty bread, dipped in *labna*, what Larissa had found out was yummy yoghurt cheese.

He'd ordered his assistants to round up the GAO trainees for a reconnaissance meeting right after he and Larissa finished breakfast. He'd insisted on having that before they started the day and, officially, the project. She'd gratefully accepted.

She'd woken up from her coma-like sleep starving. But being in such a hurry to hurtle out to work, she hadn't even considered ringing for breakfast or grabbing a bite from the guest house's overflowing fridge and kitchen. She should have insisted on grabbing something in one of the complex's five-star cafeterias and restaurants.

She'd been unable to. The last weeks had depleted her stamina and sharing meals with Faress, being pampered by him, was a pleasure she had no strength to forgo.

She bit into one of the *gorrus bel'tamr*, crumbly, unsweetened cookies baked with crunchy sesame seeds, filled with chewy dates, put the tiny hourglass crystal cup especially made for drinking Arabian coffee to her lips, gulped the bitter yet mouthwatering drink with it, the way he'd instructed her to.

She sighed at the sheer decadence of the whole experience, and finally said, "So why did you organize it?"

He sat forward, flicked a crumb from the corner of her mouth with a lingering touch, watching the predictability of her response in satisfaction as he drawled, "Because, though I always donate to GAO's efforts, I was never happy that it wasn't feasible for me to be personally involved in any of their missions. Then a friend of mine, Prince Malek Aal Hamdaan of Damhoor, did sponsor and lead such a mission in his region and the urge to go out there and reach out to people in need myself welled up again.

"But as my responsibilities as Head Surgeon here and Crown Prince elsewhere weren't about to go anywhere, I decided to go for the second-best thing. At least, second best for me. It's probably much better for GAO than having me going out there myself. They've been complaining about the range and level of skills of the volunteers they have been getting lately and I decided I'd be offering the organization a more lasting contribution by addressing those problems, training those volunteers right here, where I can continue with the rest of my responsibilities."

Judging herself reasonably recovered from his last breach of her defenses, she reached for her bowl of couscous, sprinkled it with sugar and murmured, before she took a sample to her mouth, "And you're regretting your decision now? You feel you don't have time to oversee the project?"

"I certainly don't regret it. If it wasn't something I was committed to fulfilling, it would have been enough that it brought you here for me to think it my most worthwhile idea ever."

She barely managed to gulp down the grainy richness filling her mouth instead of coughing it out.

Not missing a nuance of her reaction, he smiled. "And you know the most amazing thing? You being here is not only a godsend on a personal level, it's one on a professional one, too. You are how I'm going to be able to deal with this without dropping any of the balls I have in the air."

Telling herself she was in the presence of one of history's masters of seduction, she rasped, "H-how's that?"

"Simple. You're going to be my second-in-command. We'll work out a general plan of action, then day-to-day schedules, then when I have to tend to other chores, you'll take over, direct the other trainers, oversee particulars, deal with problems and keep a progress report on each volunteer. I'll walk back the moment I can, with you updating me on everything that transpired in my absence."

She cleared her throat around a lump of stupefaction. "And, uh…how do you know I'm qualified for such a task?"

He gave an easy shrug, the very essence of certainty. "I've worked with you, that's how I know. I saw you making life-and-death decisions in a mass-casualty situation—in the worst possible conditions. I saw you implementing an incredible range of lifesaving and trauma intervention measures. I saw how cool you are, how you dealt with unknown assistants and got the best results from each. I was considering many people for this position, but none of them fulfilled all my criteria. Then you came and solved my dilemma. You're just what I want." He paused, before he added in annihilating intimacy, "Everything that I want."

She stared at him, speechless. Not because her heart had stumbled as he'd given his reasons, stopped at his blatant double entendre. It was because she wanted to scream for *him* to stop.

Every word that declared his esteem, his desire, would only be one more lash to incense him further with their memory, their humiliation, when she had to reveal why she was really here. He'd unintentionally stacked the odds against her so that even if she threw all caution to the wind and told him now, it was already too late. It had probably been too late the moment they had laid eyes on each other and her overwhelming attraction had aroused his.

A blast of alarm severed her chaos. He was frowning.

"You're not enthusiastic about this, are you?" He sat forward, tension entering his every line, his frown deepening. "I haven't even considered your reaction, didn't think for one second that it might be unfavorable."

That was what had brought on such a spectacular scowl? She didn't even want to imagine what he'd look like really enraged.

When she couldn't bring herself to say anything,

he went on, his voice tight, for the first time a tinge of formality coloring it, "This position I'm offering you is far more involved than the one you originally signed on for, and it goes without saying it has all the privileges and compensations it deserves."

He thought she didn't want to take on the added responsibilities in the fear she wouldn't get paid extra for them?

This, while a reasonable assumption, enraged her.

She heaved herself up to her feet, scowled down at him. "You think I'm holding out for more money, Your Highness?"

He uncoiled to his feet, too, in the measured movements of a lethal predator, came within a breath to return her scowl, bending to reduce the foot difference in their heights to inches.

"What did you say?" This was a tone she hadn't heard from him yet, low, dangerous.

She didn't care. Taking a salaried position to do a job she had so wanted to volunteer for, and for such a staggering salary at that, was already too sore a point with her. But she couldn't afford to volunteer, with the baby coming. She had no idea how long she'd be able to work before giving birth, how soon afterwards she could resume working, and this job ensured a desperately needed financial security until she sorted herself out. She still felt terrible about accepting money to take part in such a great cause. He'd just pressed all her buttons and she wanted to lash back.

She said through gritted teeth, "If you think I'm bargaining for—"

He cut her off, his voice lower, more dangerous, "Not that."

She faltered now. "You mean when I said 'Your High—'"

He swooped down like an attacking eagle. She didn't have time to blink, think, to brace herself.

She didn't need to. Not against any force. His lips landed on hers in a hot, moist seal, enveloping, dissolving, his tongue delving into her open mouth in thorough possession.

She heard a sob, knew it was issuing from her only when she felt it tearing out from her very foundations, quaking them. An answering jolt swept through him, buzzing like a high-voltage current from the hands clamping her arms. She shuddered all over as if with an electric shock. He bit into her lower lip, stilled its trembling in a nip so leashed, so carnal it tore through her far more than a blood-drawing bite would have. She cried out into his mouth, opening hers wider, deepening his invasion.

Just as she felt she'd come apart, he tore his lips

away, severing their embrace with something harsh erupting from his gut, wrenching a harsher sound from hers.

The moment he freed her she stumbled back, collapsed into the nearest seat. She would have burned to ashes if she'd remained within his aura one more second.

He neared her again, bent, an imperative finger below her chin demanding her gaze. She met the blaze in his eyes, shriveled with shyness, with the scorching desire to surge up and into him again, take his lips, surrender hers, long and hard and assuaging.

"Call me 'Your Highness' again," he said, tones clipped, "and I'll stop you the same way."

And he considered that a threat? When women would fight tooth and nail to elicit even a long look from him? Was it possible he thought that was punishment?

Though maybe he did feel it *was* punishment for her. The worst possible kind. He just had no idea why it was.

He took off his jacket, threw it on the couch he'd vacated moments ago for their confrontation, tore a few of his shirt buttons open, giving her a glimpse of bronze skin sprinkled with silky black hair. Was he burning, too?

He swung towards her, dipping his hands deep in his pockets, drawing her unwilling greed and rising mortification to the evidence of the raging arousal of his formidable body.

Muttering a curse in Arabic, he took his hands out of his pockets, brought both up to his nape, linked them there, tipped his head back, stared at the ceiling for a few moments.

Then he exhaled. "I assume you have other reasons for not wanting the position I'm offering you?"

"Who said I don't want it?" she croaked, again stunned at the resilience of her speech faculties. "You just assumed that. Why? Because I didn't jump up and down right on the spot? Well, excuse me, but it takes a woman a few minutes to adjust her mindset from being one of many surgical trainers to suddenly being at the helm of the full project—at least second-in-command of said project."

His gaze sharpened on her. "You mean you accept?"

Her mouth twisted in self-deprecation. "If only not to ruin a perfect record."

One eyebrow arched at her. "And that means…?"

"It means I ended up somehow accepting all your offers, all those dizzying, blindsiding mixes of imperious commands, cajoling demands and fait accompli decisions, didn't I?"

He moved closer until his leg nudged her knee. "You are in danger of being kissed again, and this time for real."

She jumped up, put a few feet of breathable air between them. "You mean that wasn't a real kiss?" she gasped. She was done for if he ever hit her with the real deal. Which he mustn't. *Mustn't.*

And he had to go and answer her rhetorical question. "No. You'll know when I kiss you for real. From your reaction right now, you'll go up in flames, and I can't wait for them to scorch me."

Burning with mortification, she couldn't let him get the last word here. "If I've realized anything in the past couple of days, Your Highness…" She jumped out of reach when he growled and lunged for her. She put the breakfast trolley between them. "It's that no one has diagnosed you since you no doubt overwhelm everyone. So it falls to me to tell you that, while you have every reason there is to be full of yourself, it doesn't mean it's healthy. You're so addicted to your own power you should consider rehabilitation. Think of it as a sort of detox."

He stared at her in stupefaction.

Just as she thought she'd stepped over the line,

he threw his head back, exposed her again to what had to be the most fantastic sight on earth. Him in the grips of uncontrollable mirth.

"Ya Ullah..." He tried to speak between helpless guffaws. "*Entee mozth'helah*—you're just incredible. If I'm addicted then you're definitely the cure, *ya'yooni*."

She bit her tongue so she wouldn't ask what *ya'yooni* meant.

"I'm glad you find my psychoanalysis so entertaining," she mumbled, struggling with arrhythmia, rephrasing his earlier similar comment. "Just the reaction I was after."

He stalked to her again, his intention of giving her that *real* kiss blasting off him.

She held out a hand. "Faress...please, don't." That slowed him down. But he kept coming, his face alight with such passion that it made agitated words spill from her lips. "You—you probably think I was just spouting prudent-on-a-first-meeting modesty that wasn't meant to last a second meeting. And from women's reaction to you—hell, from *my* reaction—you have every right to think this. So, yes, if you want an admission, you overwhelm me. But I don't want you to. If we're going to work together as closely as you suggest, please, stop trying to ratchet up the intimacy between us. If you don't…" She faltered for a second then blurted out, "I'll have to leave!"

That made him stop, evaporated all heat from his face.

A long moment later, during which she felt he'd given her a full body and mind scan, solemn, almost grim, he muttered, "Is there someone else?"

"What? No, *no*…" The denial burst out of her before she gave herself a mental smack. Why was she so anxious to deny the charge? She rushed on, in a less fretful tone this time, "But that's not the only reason a woman—"

He cut her off, tension visibly draining out of him. "That's the only reason I consider. If there's no prior claim to your emotions and fidelity, no other reason is good enough to stop me from claiming you for myself."

"Good enough according to whom?" she groaned.

He gave her a new look, full of reason and open-mindedness. "Convince me how good your reasons are. Tell me."

Tell him? Yeah, sure.

Instead she tried to search for something feasible to explain the reluctance he knew had nothing to do with what she really wanted. Finding nothing even remotely so, she groaned. "You are going to make me leave, aren't you?"

His eyes flared. "I would do anything to stop you leaving."

"Then, please, Faress—I can't handle this kind of pressure."

In answer, he reached for her and all resolution and self-preservation ebbed out of her. He kept his embrace undemanding and it only stormed through her defenses more.

He smoothed a gentle hand over her hair, in soothing, hypnotic strokes. "I am sorry, *ya jameelati,* if I am going too fast for you. But whatever hit us both, my reaction is not to struggle against it, but to rush to the very center of its overpowering gravity towards you. It's the way I'm made. But to let you get your bearings, I'll slow down."

"I want you to *stop*, Faress."

"No." This was said with the most indulgent of smiles. And was there any wonder? With her asking him to stop in a breathless quaver that all but begged him to brush her demand aside, give her what she really craved, more and more of him. "I will slow down. This is all I can promise you."

"Faress…"

"I won't be near you and not say and do what your nearness inspires and arouses me to say and do. But you will be the one to tell me you're ready for the next step. Now give me your decision. Will you stay? Will you be my right hand?"

She nodded, then groaned. "Now I know how you run a country. You compel everyone to do what you want as if by magic, and have them totally convinced and happy doing it, too."

His smile was an amalgam of relief and mischief, yet another in his fibrillation-inducing repertoire. "I don't exactly run the country single-handedly, *ya helwah*," he teased. "We do have a king and a thousand royals around. But where I do run things, like in this complex, the trick is to know what everyone wants that works with what I want then put people where I think they'll fulfill that best. This way everyone ends up working extra hard because it's in their best interests too, freeing me to concentrate on what I'm best at, being a surgeon, and everybody ends up happy."

She sighed. "And from what I've seen of the complex, your strategy is yielding spectacular results. Something this effective just has to be wicked."

"Oh, I'm wicked. Wickedly effective." He gave her cheek the softest pinch. "Now, before I jinx myself so everything I touch devolves into anarchy, let's get to work, number one."

* * *

They got to work. For the next few days they made up their schedule, adjusted it a dozen times before finally settling into a steady, productive, if mind-numbingly exhausting rhythm.

She'd at first thought the whole thing too daunting a task. Faress was offering such an unprecedented opportunity it seemed everyone who'd ever wanted to volunteer had found this the best time to do so. Three hundred and fifty trainees were way more than she'd expected. And their role was to prepare them, mostly medical professionals who'd drifted away from practice with enough updated medical and surgical skills to function in the field.

It had seemed more daunting when she'd shot her mouth off and, instead of arguing with her, Faress had entrusted her with picking the fourteen she'd directly train. The others she only oversaw in rotation with him over the other two dozen trainers' shoulders.

Now she was with the four she judged could move into a real trauma surgery scenario. The other ten of her team were watching from the Plexiglas-walled, soundproofed observation rooms ringing the OR a level up. When the surgery began, their viewing experience would include monitors transmitting the recording of the surgery from video cameras in the hi-tech ceiling mechanisms, as well as through endoscope-mounted ones. Later they'd each have a DVD of the surgery to study, then there'd be discussions of what had gone on, alternate ways to have done each step in various conditions of preparedness, and when hopefully everything had gone well, discuss what couldn't have and what to do in each scenario.

"Can anybody tell me why Es-sayed Hamed El-Etaibi here..." Larissa gestured towards their sedated patient, a dark, overweight man who looked ferociously upset even in sedation "...though he took a thirty-foot fall to break both femurs in a dozen places, and as he yelled before morphine dissipated his pain and consciousness, on his birthday too, is still a lucky man?"

Larissa looked from one of her assistants to another as they surrounded the OR table.

"He's lucky because he's still alive?" Helal Othman quipped.

She gave the lanky forty-year-old with a hawk's face and sharpness an assessing glance. He could do better than that. He was brilliant and had been the first one she'd picked as best suited for involved trauma surgery training. He was a Damhoorian general surgeon who'd taken a sharp detour into the stock market over ten years ago and who'd decided he wanted to get back into the medical world, if only as a volunteer. But he was also a clown and he couldn't pass up any opportunity to make a joke.

She smirked at him. "Any more medically specific reason to consider him lucky, other than steady life signs?"

Before a sheepish Helal could come up with a more serious answer, a drawl broke out from behind her. "Because he's got you working on him?"

Faress. Oh, God. She didn't jump. Somehow.

"Uh, it remains to be seen if that's lucky." She turned to Faress, hoping it wasn't too apparent she wanted to whoop with pleasure that he'd come after all. She'd joined him for his morning surgery list as she now did every day, only starting her training schedule after the lunch-break when he'd always done his best to join her. Today he'd said not to expect him.

But he was here. *Here.* Walking in those leashed-power steps, making the shapeless blue surgical gown look like the height of virile haute couture.

She somehow managed to murmur what she thought a reasonably cool and professional, "Glad you could make it." Then before she made a fool of herself by absorbing his sight like a starstruck idiot, she turned to her trainees. "But he's really lucky for a specific reason, which I hope you figure out, or I'll know that my course on 'Gift horses in trauma and the thankful trauma surgeon' has entered one ear and exited from the other."

Her four assistants hadn't recovered from Faress's entrance yet. But besides the awed stares, they were also casting curious glances from him to her. Speculation about the nature of their relationship was running rampant throughout the complex.

At last, her oldest assistant, Patrick Dempsey, an Australian sixty-three-year-old grizzly bear with a gooey center, an obstetrician who'd decided to retire, then continue his life as a volunteer, seeking training in the field of surgery that had always fascinated him, said, "Let's see…the first gift horse is when we're certain what a trauma case *does* have, no matter how bad, since in trauma it's always worse if we're not sure. In Mr El-Etaibi's case, what he does have is a diaphragmatic rupture…"

Larissa cocked her head at him. "I only *said* he does."

His salt-and-pepper bearded jaw fell open. "He doesn't?"

She shrugged. "You tell me if I was telling the truth."

"Well, you were," Patrick started. "All his signs—"

She cut in, "Were mostly inconclusive and misleading."

"Yeah, that's true," he conceded. "But his investigations—"

She cut in again. "Abnormalities in X-rays aren't conclusive in diaphragmatic rupture without abdominal organs in the chest cavity. CT and MRI are also inaccurate in such conditions."

"So you didn't diagnose him?" Patrick looked stymied. "You were just testing to see if we'd know that you couldn't have?"

She shrugged again. "You tell me."

"You didn't diagnose him." That was the only woman around, Anika Jansen, a thirty-five-year-old Dutch former surgical nurse, with tons of theoretical and practical surgical knowledge. "You have a strong suspicion and that's why you're performing a video-assisted thoracoscopy. If your suspicion is right, you'll turn the diagnostic procedure into a surgical one and repair the tear."

Larissa beamed at the lovely blonde, proud of her knowledge and reasoning powers, and simply glad to have another woman and such a kindred soul around. Though all the men were perfect gentlemen, too much testosterone got to her sometimes.

"That is a perfect answer," Larissa said. "And the course of action you should adopt in almost all suspected diaphragmatic rupture cases if at all possible…" She paused with an apologetic glance at Anika. "But this answer isn't perfect here, since I *am* certain what he's suffering from. VAT will only have a surgical role here. So what does he have? And how did I know? Take another look at his history and investigations and tell me."

They shuffled to gather over the patient's file, leaving her without the safety net of their focus and all alone in Faress's.

He moved towards her, shrinking the gigantic hall, emptying it of air. And that when he only came to stand in her first assistant's position across Hamed. He kept his distance in public, physically. Not that it stopped people from speculating. It was the vibes they generated. She sometimes felt they were tangible. It was impossible for others not to feel them.

He let go of her eyes to sweep his over their patient, his expert gaze missing nothing. A murmur brought a nurse streaking forward to leaf through a copy of Hamed's file for him.

"*Shokrun*," he murmured after a few absorbed moments and the nurse closed the file and moved away. His eyes went back to the patient. "That's one angry man. A stable one who can still take a turn for the catastrophic. A baffling enough case to give your team's clinical knowledge a trial by fire. Great choice." He raised his eyes, the usual intimacy filling them still something she couldn't face. "I found myself unexpectedly free and came over. It's only fair to hold your hand on your first big outing with your charges when you hold mine every day in my lists."

"As if I do," she breathed, her mind filling with images of all the times he'd held her hand, scorched it in caresses and kisses. "As if you need anyone to hold your hand."

"You do, and I do need an intuitive, fluent, resourceful first assistant. And you're the best I've ever had."

Now she was in danger of spontaneously combusting. Or would that be arson? Since he was setting her on fire?

"Uh—right." She cast blind eyes away from his entrancing face. "Anyway, that's no big outing. Even had they been trauma surgeons, with the staggering advances in the time they've been away from practice, I wouldn't have risked their involvement yet. As it is, they're just observing and assisting in minor stuff."

"You're still the only surgical trainer who thinks her team ready for even that in only two weeks."

"It's because I'm the only surgical trainer who was lucky enough to pick the cream of the crop of trainees." He gave her that indulgent smile he always did when she bragged about her team's skills. Her heart responded with the usual kick against her ribs. "I can't believe it's been two weeks already."

His eyes blazed a few degrees hotter. "They feel like two hours. And two years. Either way, they passed like a dream."

Not where their work was concerned, they hadn't. The dream was every excitement-filled, emotion-charged moment with him. And that he meant the same about being with her…

"So you think they'll solve your puzzle? You haven't confused them too much?"

His murmur made her blink. His smile made her certain she'd been looking at him with her thoughts written all over her face.

She cleared her throat. "I'm confident a good look at the facts will lead them to the truth."

He gave her team an assessing look. "And you know what? I now share your confidence.

You're blessed with the ability of gauging people's worth. I for one thought Helal, while brilliant, was too much of an undisciplined clown, and Patrick, while methodical and thorough, was too much of an uncooperative grouch. I had reservations about the rest, too. But your evaluation was correct. They're topping all theoretical training charts, and if their practical simulation scores keep up, every one of the fourteen you picked to train yourself will be the first we hand back to GAO with our seal of approval."

Heat rushed to her head at his validation. She'd felt a similar rush when, in spite of his skepticism, he'd so graciously let her make her picking decisions.

She'd agonized over the ones she'd picked. As she was only twenty-seven, they were all much older than her. She'd only ever trained interns and junior residents at most her age or a bit older.

Faress had declared age was irrelevant, that they'd recognize ability and follow the lead of experience. That glowing testimony had only made her even more scared she'd fall flat on her face.

She'd started her basic surgical skills refresher course with an unhealthy dose of trepidation, only for their terrific attitude to dispel it in an hour. They'd made a great team from day one.

At her silence he pouted. "You won't jump on my concession?"

Her mouth twisted, mostly at her reaction to his pout. "You think you're the only one who doesn't indulge in I-told-you-sos?" At the flare in his eyes she rushed to add, "Not that I'm not glad you think they'll be the first to be ready. As long as you don't expect this to be within the next two and a half months."

"Of course not. You can take as long as you deem necessary to get them ready for the field."

There he went again, talking as if it went without saying that she'd stay way longer than her contracted three months!

But she couldn't even dream of that. She was counting down to one of two moments, both leading to her departure. Either she confronted Faress and his family over her baby and left, leaving them to consider how to take part in his life, or she didn't and left before her pregnancy became visible. She couldn't even bear to think of a confrontation with Faress over it.

She was searching desperately for a way to avoid what he was after, an assurance she'd stay indefinitely, when her assistants walked back to flank both her and Faress and saved her.

Obviously displeased that he hadn't obtained

what he wanted, at least to her hypersensitive senses, Faress tore his gaze away from her, turned it on them. “Well, don’t leave me in suspense. Why is *Es-sayed* Hamed deemed lucky by your illustrious trainer?”

“Let’s present the first gift horse, Dr. Faress,” Anika said, fluttering like all females fluttered in his presence. “He does have a diaphragmatic tear. Larissa knew that from his paradoxical breathing. With no multiple rib fractures, the only other reason could be rupture and paralysis of one side of his diaphragm.”

“And the reason he’s lucky,” Helal put in confidently, “is that it’s on the left side, where tears are usually isolated.”

He gave her a look that said, *You’re right to be proud of them*. Out loud he said, “I’m impressed. Truly. Well done.”

As her assistants shuffled their pleasure at his praise, Larissa thought she should end this before his agitating effect rendered them useless, as he almost did her.

“And while *Es-sayed* Hamed is nowhere within the danger zone time-wise,” she said, “always get on with your intervention while you have plenty of time on your side.”

She turned to Dr. Tarek, who’d become her

constant anesthetist companion. "Switch to general anesthesia, please, Dr. Tarek. Turn him to his right side, please, Patrick, Tom."

As they did as she directed, Faress came to stand behind her, looking over her shoulder as he'd been doing each time he wasn't the primary surgeon while she assisted, or vice versa.

She took a steadying breath, made the first incision between the ribs, introduced the tiny fiber-optic thoracoscope through it, all the time detailing her technique for her viewers. She advanced the stapler through another incision. Soon she visualized the tear and started to staple it shut.

As they watched the injury being sealed on the monitors, she felt Faress's readiness to help if she needed him, felt his bolstering presence enveloping her.

And though she told herself she was being maudlin and stupid, questions kept revolving in her mind.

When she left, what kind of injury would tearing herself from all that, from him, inflict?

And what would it take to seal it?

CHAPTER FIVE

"KEEP walking. I'm abducting you."

Faress watched Larissa jump and whirl around, her eyes snapping up, slamming into his pseudo-menacing ones.

Elation fizzed in his blood as emotions chased away the melancholy she lapsed into when she thought herself safe from scrutiny.

He was now certain she'd recently suffered a loss. Too huge to come to terms with, too raw to talk about.

But instead of making him obey his need to tear down her barriers, satisfy his painful curiosity and absorb all the pain she harbored, it made him hold back, in respect for the sanctity of her suffering, until she gathered enough stamina to seek his solace.

But *enough.* It wasn't time she needed. It was him. Losing herself in his arms would be the best medicine. Tonight he'd end the frustration, start her healing. He had a night of magic planned for them.

Though if she insisted it was still too soon, he'd have to wait…

He believed he wouldn't have to.

She stumbled back a step, leaned on the wall.

"I said keep walking, *ya jameelati*," he drawled again, coaxing, hunger turning his voice into a bass rasp.

"Aren't you afraid that with the advance warning I'd make a run for it?" she breathed, her eyes helplessly clinging to his lips.

He put a hand on each side of her head. "You know you don't want to escape me. Now we'll walk out to the airfield and I'll fly you to my hideaway. You haven't been to Bidalya until you've spent a night in our desert, under the full moon."

Her breath came faster now, the rise and fall of her perfect breasts pouring magma into his veins, his head flooding with images of suckling them, branding them, devouring them.

"Full moon?" The strident murmur seemed for her own ears only. "I arrived on a full moon."

And how he remembered. It had been one of his theories that day, that the full moon had had a role in his hyper-reactions. But when they'd become even more so on exposure to her, he'd known. The only magic had been hers. Her.

"Yes. You've been with me for four glorious weeks."

Next second she was at his feet in a heap.

It took him another second for the blast of fright to detonate in his mind. *"Larissa!"*

He swooped down on her, his hands flailing over her, all medical knowledge evaporating at seeing her limp and senseless.

He barely registered the gathering mob around him, felt nothing but panic suffocating him, the need to restore her almost rupturing his skull.

"Dr. Faress, let us take care of her."

"No." He roared at whoever had dared make the suggestion. Then he was scooping her up in his arms and running.

She had to be all right. She had to be.

He couldn't live otherwise…

Larissa opened her eyes. It took her a moment to realize what had happened, where she was.

She'd fainted. For the first time ever. And she couldn't *believe* where Faress had her now.

She was in the new multi-million-dollar IC, the first patient in it, hooked to half a dozen monitors. He was leaning over her, his eyes drilling anxiety into her. And he was about to plunge a needle into her vein. No doubt to extract blood for investigations. *No.*

She yanked her arm away, scrambled up in bed, started snatching off leads.

"Lie down, Larissa," Faress growled. "And give me your arm."

She shook her head. "I'm fine. Really."

"You're not fine or you wouldn't have fainted. And what's this? The fearless surgeon afraid of a needle prick?"

She swung her legs off the bed. She had to get out of there. "Aren't you going overboard over a slight fainting spell?"

"You were out for fifteen minutes. I don't call that slight."

She attempted a wavering smile. "Maybe it was an act to escape your intended abduction."

He gave her a disparaging pout. "Even if I believed you can act to save your life, which I don't, you can't fake tachycardia. Your heart was hurtling at 170 per minute." His eyes flared at the memory, his voice thickening. "You scared the hell out of me."

Her heart hurtled once more at his impassioned confession.

She escaped his attempt to make her lie down again. "My blood sugar must have suddenly dropped," she gasped. "Stop fussing, *please*."

He unfolded to his full height, scowled down at her. "You didn't eat lunch when I was called away, did you?" She grabbed at his explanation, nodded. "And you've been skipping meals every time I didn't make sure you ate. You *are* losing weight."

"Isn't that every woman's dream?"

"It shouldn't be yours. You can't improve on perfection."

She coughed in distressed incredulity. "That hyperbole aside, if I ate every meal the way you have me eating, you'll have to roll me around before long. I got busy and I thought I could skip a meal. Evidently not. So, I promise, no skipping meals from now on. Can I go now?"

"No, you can't. You're staying the night. As for being too busy to eat, that tears it. You're working too hard. I'm cutting your workload to half."

"Now, be reasonable, Faress. I'm only working eight hours per day. What will I do with myself if you cut them to four?"

"You mean while waiting for me to come to you? Rest, read, shop. You have carte blanche to do anything in the kingdom."

Her lips twisted. "That's too generous, Your Highness, but—"

He swooped down on her, his lips clamping hers in all-out possession. Just as she sobbed, surrendered, let him surge inside her mouth, devour her, his pager beeped.

He withdrew, breathing harshly. "You're *not* saved by the beep. Leave the glucose line in and eat the food I'll send you. All of it. I'm returning as soon as I'm done. And I'm staying in the complex overnight, so don't think you can slink away."

With one last fierce kiss, he let her go and rose to his feet. Larissa's eyes clung to him until he disappeared then they squeezed shut as she trembled with the reprieve.

She couldn't have borne him finding out she was pregnant that way. She had to tell him herself. If she told him at all.

And she'd been just thinking how her first trimester had passed smoothly! Then he'd reminded her she'd been here four weeks and she'd read his intention for tonight to be *the* night and everything had gone blank, no doubt seeking to escape the confrontation she was now dreading.

As it was, her faint *had* solved the immediate problem. He was so concerned, his plans to push their relationship to the next level were seemingly on hold.

"You're pregnant, aren't you?"

Her eyes snapped open, her gaze slamming up at the whispered words in shock.

She only found Patrick, standing above her, his face the essence of kindness. She groaned. Leave it to an obstetrician with over three decades' experience to recognize her condition. She could only nod.

"And you don't want…anyone to know." She heard Faress in place of that "anyone" loud and clear. She nodded again. He sat down beside her. "What are you doing about your antenatal checks?"

She let out a tremulous breath. "I haven't been getting any. I'm afraid if I do, it would get around."

"Not if I'm your obstetrician, it won't. Let's set up a schedule right now. And get that first check under way."

"Oh, Patrick." She clung to his hand with a sob. "Thank you."

He squeezed her hand and gave her a huge wink. "Oh, you won't thank me when you see the list of dos and don'ts I have for you."

A week later, on the first day Faress allowed Larissa to work a full day, she was in her office, that gigantic, postmodern space he'd allocated to her, surrounded by her team who used it as their hangout, when Helal walked in.

"Did you hear about the latest human rights breach the good king of Bidalya committed yesterday?"

Larissa's heart took a now-familiar plunge to the

pit of her stomach. Not another rumor, she groaned inwardly.

"I wonder where you hear these things." Anika raised her head from her laptop and mumbled, "I haven't met one Bidalyan who has anything bad to say about King Qassem."

Helal gave her a pitying glance. "You haven't met Bidalyans, you've met people who work in this complex. You think they'd speak out against their worshipped employer's father?"

"I do go out after work, you know?" Anika smirked.

"And it doesn't surprise you no one has anything derogatory to say about the king? Where in the world does a ruler have his people's complete admiration and support?"

"In your country?" Anika shot back.

"It's Prince Malek who had that, and he abdicated. Our regent is fine, but he isn't perfect. And we can say that in Damhoor, privately or publicly, and not get arrested."

Anika gave him a ridiculing glance. "So every Bidalyan who has criticized the king has been arrested?"

"Many have. The king is intolerant and senile, and hasn't heard the twenty-first century is well under way."

"Let's say he's no angel," Tom Gerard countered. He was an American neurosurgeon who after a twelve-year rehabilitation following a near-fatal accident had decided to return to medicine as a volunteer. His ordeals had tempered him with infinite tolerance and insight. "But what ruler hasn't been accused of that? Here I can see no reason for the sweeping majority of Bidalyans to be dissatisfied with theirs. The average Bidalyan lives like a king in a country that's a marvel of modern advances and constant development."

"So they should shut up when their rights are breached if they don't toe the line?" Helal shot back. "And it isn't him who's responsible for all the security and prosperity. It's Prince Faress and his modernizing, innovating team of royal cousins. The king is just an old despot Prince Faress barely keeps in check nationally and keeps hidden internationally."

"Just don't let him hear you say that." Patrick slapped Helal on the back. "Dr. Faress, I mean. Calling him *Prince* Faress here."

Larissa couldn't let one more word or speculation add to her turmoil and indecision.

She got to her feet. "How about you keep your crusading powers for the areas of the world that need it, Helal? *When* I whip you into a good enough trauma surgeon, and when Bidalya, where we're all subsidized guests, salvages the other areas of your surgical prowess? And how about I find out if your unquestionable knowledge extends to damage control surgery?"

Everyone burst out laughing at Helal's chagrin before he joined in then proceeded to make an outrageous joke of the whole situation all through their session. Larissa went along with the rampant teasing, if only to cover up her tumult.

Though she'd stopped Helal short, her own information-gathering had validated his words *and* her initial fear of Jawad's father. Every source said that while the king wisely presented Faress to the outside world as Bidalya's advanced, peace-advocating, benevolent front, let him and the younger generation of his royal family forge Bidalya's foreign policy and take it to its current prosperity, Faress couldn't be everywhere, was engrossed in his medical role. A lot slipped under his radar, while the king still ruled absolutely and sometimes most unwisely in many internal affairs.

So when…if…she revealed her secret and the king's reaction was worse than anything she'd ever feared from the reasonable, refined man Faress was, would Faress be able to counteract it? And even if he did, was it wise to let that kind of man be the baby's grandfather, the one with the most say and sway in his life? Could she possibly tell Faress only? What would that achieve? Except alienation from him and nothing at all for the baby? Without the king's knowledge, Jawad's heritage wouldn't be passed on.

Despondent, more undecided than ever, she staggered out at the end of the session. *Oh, God, Faress, where are you?*

He'd never been away longer than four hours at a time. But yesterday he hadn't spent the evening with her, hadn't taken her home. And today he hadn't escorted her to work. He'd canceled his morning list, had told her to substitute it with her training session. He'd called her at one p.m. to say he'd be a bit later. It was now four p.m. That made it twenty-four hours since she'd last seen him. She still kept expecting, *hoping* he'd materialize like he always did, her heart dropping a beat out of every three.

He didn't.

She entered the ward where they shared scheduling cases each day on dragging feet, grief hitting her the hardest it had since she'd set foot in Bidalya, almost doubling her over.

Faress had been giving her no chance to dwell on how lost she felt without Claire, her confidante, advisor and the surrogate mother who'd made losing both their parents when she'd been only twelve survivable. The roller-coaster of emotions he'd plunged her into had distracted her from burning with rage at fate for depriving her, depriving the world of such an incredible being. But all it had taken had been a day away from him for her to revert to her misery before she'd laid eyes on him.

Deprived of his borrowed vitality and stability at a time when the support of preoccupation was temporarily removed, memories, anguish hit her with the force of an eviscerating blow.

Just as she stumbled with it, another thought struck her, sending her first taste of real nausea welling up her throat.

What if Faress had decided she wasn't worth more of his time or attention?

He'd kept his promise after all, had slowed down. Not that she felt he had. If she'd thought he'd overwhelmed her at first, she should have reserved judgment a bit longer. He was an unbelievable amalgam of old-world chivalry and contemporary sophistication and charisma, all entrenched in true superiority and profound benevolence. What she'd seen of him then had been but a taste of a humbling human being.

But maybe he'd been withdrawing, not slowing

down. And if this was true, was today the beginning of the end?

She should be hoping it was.

As long as he pursued her, she was trapped, couldn't find an opening to even broach the subject of the baby. But if he was cooling now, he might develop the detachment that would avail her of an objective hearing. Her one chance was if he was forgetting about her in the heat of another conquest and…

She couldn't bear thinking he was forgetting about her.

But he *wasn't*. She had last week to prove it! And just yesterday he'd still been lavishing passion and hunger, respect and admiration on her…

So how could she confront him, pulverize all that?

Oh, God, she'd trapped herself on a one-way road to damnation the day she'd withheld the truth from him.

Pressure built inside her, desperate for an outlet, until she prayed her skull would burst. It didn't, the pressure not finding release even in the tears that clogged her eyes.

Oh, Claire. What shall I do?

As if in answer to her plea, an answer boomed in her head.

Tell him the truth. Now. *Come what may.*

Withholding it any more meant sinking deeper into the unintentional deception, ending up looking far worse in his eyes once it came out. And it had to come out. She owed it to him that she told him all, her situation, his brother's fate and his unborn nephew's existence. She could only pray he'd understand, be lenient with her, kind to his flesh and blood.

Taking several deep breaths until she started feeling light-headed, she turned around—and almost stumbled.

He was walking through the ward's door, his gaze catching hers at once with *that* look in his eyes. The look to dive into and never resurface from. The look that told her all her hopeful dread had been unfounded, that instead of cooling he was now like a heat-seeking missile, locked onto his course and unswerving.

Except if she told him something drastic. Like the truth.

But until she did, he wasn't stopping. Conquerors of his caliber only became unwavering with a difficult target.

She stood transfixed, watching him eliminating the distance between them, grateful for the tiny favor of being in public. It was only there he didn't touch her, his aversion to public displays of affection a personal predilection, she was sure, not one imposed by the conservative culture or his status.

Then he spoke and she almost collapsed at his feet.

"Did you miss me, *ya jameelati*?"

Faress heard the gruffness of his voice, had no control over it, didn't want to control it.

Why should he? He wanted her to hear it, see it, how he'd hungered for a sight of her after an endless day of deprivation.

He hadn't expected an answer to the question he'd used for a caress, an embrace. But she gave him one, an overcome nod as her eyes stormed through an unprecedented array of hues.

Elation stormed from his depths. She'd missed him. Like he'd missed her. He couldn't believe how he'd missed her.

But then again, he believed nothing more. Her spell had been tightening over his senses from that first look. She wasn't only the female who appealed to everything male in him, she was the doctor whose skills and work ethic enthralled the doctor, the wit and mind that spellbound the intellectual, and the overall character who'd earned the admiration and respect of the man.

He was used to recognizing talent and assigning responsibility to the capable. But he'd never had anyone surpass his expectations like she had, never counted on anyone as unquestioningly as he'd come to count on her.

From the moment he'd unloaded most of his burden of the project onto her shoulders, she'd amazed him. She'd taken his plans and tightened them up, kept fine-tuning them. The project was turning into a great success and it wouldn't have without her. She kept surprising him, keeping up with him like no one ever had, his most valuable surgical partner to date, enhancing his efficiency, saving him untold time and effort while saving priceless lives and preparing others for doing the same. He delighted in their intuitive rapport and the complementing array of skills they possessed and exchanged.

Then there were the precious personal times that gave him his first taste of true happiness.

He'd at first surrendered to the immense emotions she evoked in him without trying to identify them. It had taken her collapse, feeling dread tearing at his insides, despair at imagining a life without her, to know what they were. That transporting, transfiguring malady called love.

Instead of being appalled by his diagnosis, he was elated. Yes, this was love. And it wasn't a malady but an enhancement of life. And it had claimed him whole when he'd always thought it a fiction, when he'd been resigned he'd one day wed for duty.

Now he'd wed for love. And who more worthy than her to bestow his heart, faith and honor on? She was a being without equal, and he would be the proudest man on earth to call her his, to pledge himself hers. No matter the opposition. Or the price.

He now stopped himself with all his will so he wouldn't cleave her to him. He'd never been one for exhibiting emotions. Now he realized he'd never had any to exhibit. She'd changed that. In private, he lavished intimacies on her. In public he barely held them back, so he wouldn't compromise her image as a lady and a professional or her status as his deputy.

But a day apart had turned the certainty of his emotions into urgency, made him unable to wait to proclaim them, to draw her admission of equal involvement with him.

He touched her, powerless to stay away, needing to absorb her tiredness and all her troubles. He needed *her*, must have her, soon, and for ever. He groaned with it all. "And how I missed you."

Larissa lurched at Faress's touch, at his words, raised her wavering gaze to his, and the tears that had been accumulating inside her almost burst out under pressure.

This was the last look of warmth and craving and indulgence, and, oh, God, respect, trust, untainted by doubts and resentment, she'd ever see in his eyes. She drowned in it, flayed herself with it, then inhaled the breath to fuel the words that would deprive her of it all…

"*Somow'w'El Ameer* Faress*!*"

The shout shot through her, severing the last of her control.

Worry flared in Faress's eyes at her shuddering reaction and he tightened his grip on her arm. Next second the man who'd shouted for him almost barreled into him, snatching his focus away.

Faress swung around to him, took hold of him to steady him, give him an anxious shake. "Speak, *ya rejjal*!"

The man burst out in agitated Arabic and Larissa felt each word jolt through Faress like a bullet. Her anxiety surged with his until she cried out, "What is it?"

Faress turned to her, his whole face working. "It's my sister Ghadah and my niece, Jameelah—they've been in a helicopter crash."

CHAPTER SIX

THE trip on board Faress's flying hospital to the accident scene was a nightmare. As much of a nightmare as the trip Larissa had made just eight weeks ago, to her own sister's accident scene. The only difference was that on that trip she'd already known what to expect. Her sister had already been dead. They'd been certain.

She'd still torn through the bleak, freezing roads with one idea filling her head. That they'd been wrong, that her sister was only gravely injured, her life signs so weak they'd hadn't been able to detect them. That she could still save her.

They hadn't been wrong. Her sister's death had been instantaneous. Larissa had wondered ever since if she'd meant it to be, to make sure Larissa would have no chance to pull her back from death's jaws, like she had countless trauma victims.

But Faress's sister and niece were still alive. They could still save them. *If* they reached them in time.

She clamped her jaw against yet another geyser of debilitating frustration.

It had been fifteen minutes since they'd taken off. They were supposed to reach the crash scene in fifteen more. But each second as she'd watched Faress go through hell was a brand-new definition of the word. The need to ward off his anguish, to help his loved ones was making every second a lifetime. It wasn't making it any more endurable knowing her role would come later.

Her blood had chilled in helplessness as she'd watched the rescue efforts via satellite feed on half a dozen monitors in the communications cabin, keeping totally still so as not to distract Faress.

He hadn't paused for breath ever since they'd come on board, barking constant directions, orchestrating the efforts of the teams extricating the victims from the wreck. She'd lived his distress as Ghadah and Jameelah had been, by necessity, the last ones to be extracted, reliving her own horror and agony on watching her sister's lifeless body being pulled out from the twisted hulk of metal that had been her car.

Both the pilot and Ghadah's assistant were suffering from minor injuries. But the co-pilot was dead, of what had clearly been instantly fatal multiple injuries. Ghadah's and Jameelah's injuries were life-threatening. It was a small mercy both weren't suffering from significant external injuries. She couldn't stand to imagine he could have seen his loved ones like she'd seen her sister.

His voice was rising, developing a terrible, jagged edge that tore across her hyper-extended nerves, the bellows of a cornered lion, of a man losing his mind, as he directed those installing initial lifesaving measures. If she was going crazy, needing to be taking care of them herself, she could only imagine what he was going through, and only because she'd once been there herself. It was unbearable, feeling his suffering.

She looked out of the window at the dunes racing past, stretching to the horizon, the declining sun melding their variegated magnificence with that of azure skies tinged with all the hues of the spectrum to paint a landscape of unforgiving beauty.

Tears accumulated behind the dam of all that stopped her from giving in to their release. Foremost was her need to be Faress's strong right hand in his life's darkest hour. She wouldn't let the echoes of her own ordeal render her less than perfectly useful to him.

"Larissa." Faress's call brought her out of her struggles, dissipating any weakness, had her beside him in a second, ready for anything, his to command. He took her shoulders in a steely vise, looked down at her with eyes gone wild with foreboding.

"You'll see to Jameelah and I'll see to Ghadah. The moment either of us stabilizes their charge and is sure she can hold for even minutes without intervention, we'll go to help the other with the less stable one."

She clutched his arms, her heart torn at seeing him so shaken, so vulnerable. "We'll save them, Faress," she pledged.

He gritted his teeth, gave a curt nod, before he drew her to him, ground stiff, trembling lips to her forehead.

The moment the helicopter descended, he let her go, exploded around and through its hundred-foot length to its door at the tail, shouting orders left and right. He knocked the door open, jumped out of the helicopter when it was still some feet off the ground. At the last moment before she jumped out in his wake she remembered.

She couldn't. She could fall, hurt the baby.

With a bursting heart she waited as the door that turned into four steps whacked the ground as the chopper came to a standstill on the ground. She negotiated the steps then ran across what felt like an impeding sea of powdered gold.

In seconds she was beside Faress who'd fallen to his knees between his unconscious sister and niece.

At her first look at them her heart convulsed, her pain at seeing them this way soaring for their distressing resemblance to Faress.

Ghadah was what her name proclaimed her to be, a beauty, Faress's feminine equivalent, a statuesque, queenly woman of overpowering femininity. Jameelah lived up to her name, too. Beautiful. Clearly Faress's flesh and blood, what his daughter would look like one day…

She bit her lip hard, drawing blood as she swooped down on Jameelah. Faress had forbidden intubation attempts. With both maximum suspicion head and neck injury cases, he couldn't risk anyone less skilled than them handling it. She wasn't waiting until they were inside the helicopter.

Faress validated her decision, rasped, "We intubate here."

Without missing a beat they both reached for intubation instruments, had Ghadah and Jameelah intubated within minutes, the difficult procedures proving his fear had been justified.

Then each raced into an initial survey, exchanged

clipped, shorthand trauma findings, each painting a grave diagnosis and a possible bleak prognosis.

In minutes he raised his eyes to her, his urgency making him terse. "Let's get them to surgery."

Then everything overlapped. Securing Jameelah for the transfer, running beside her and then ahead, directing assistants, installing her in the fully equipped surgical station, connecting her to a dozen monitors, injecting her with contrast material, watching radiographic images, getting a definitive diagnosis.

All the time it felt she was sharing every second with Faress, her lungs burning on the same bated breath, her throat closing on the same mounting desperation as he rushed through the same sequence with Ghada, but reaching a far worse diagnosis.

After resuscitation, she left her assistants performing crucial investigations on Jameelah and raced to his side.

Faress snatched a look up at her before returning feverish eyes to Ghada, his hands a blur as he instituted one measure after another, calibrated one machine then the next, obtaining more and more readings and images.

Larissa gave him the report his single burning glance had asked for. "Jameelah has blunt abdominal aorta injury, consistent with a seat-belt injury, has a contained if growing pseudo-aneurysm. Aggressive fluids are correcting her shock so far."

Faress's shuddering exhalation agreed with her decision to leave Jameelah to come to his aid with Ghada. Though the ten-year-old's injury could turn catastrophic, with the pseudo-aneurysm bursting and causing fatal internal hemorrhage if not controlled at once, Ghada was the one in graver danger right now.

Unable to speak, Faress's agonized gaze led hers to the monitor transmitting images from an overhead X-ray machine.

Larissa barely caught back a cry. Ghada had four pulverized thoracic vertebrae!

Even before she snatched burning eyes from the catastrophic injury to images detailing Ghada's thoracic and intracranial injuries that made her a multi-trauma nightmare, Larissa had seen enough to plunge her into despair. Whatever they did now, Ghada would probably be crippled for the rest of her life.

But that was no consideration right now. They had to save her life. And then her spinal cord might be intact. Her lack of reflexes on initial survey could be transient spinal shock. They had to take care of the immediate dangers.

"We'll deal with the thoracic hemorrhage first?"

she asked. Faress's answer was practical, as with a face turned to stone and motions as precise as an automaton, he made his first incision between Ghada's ribs. He was going for a thoracotomy. There was no place for minimally invasive techniques here. She handed him a rib spreader, waited until he placed it then took over, needing to spare him being the one to saw his sister's chest open. He let her without a word, raised the rate of blood transfusion to maximum, demanded ten more units then suctioned what seemed to be an unending fount of blood out of Ghada's chest cavity.

They explored and repaired the lung and great vessels injuries in record time. But it seemed nothing they were doing had any effect. Ghada's vital signs deteriorated steadily.

They rushed through closure, immediately turned to her subdural hematoma evacuation. They'd gone through scalp and skull opening, were working in tandem like a perfectly oiled machine, suctioning blood, irrigating clots and cauterizing bleeding vessels when Faress suddenly spoke, his voice as thick and ghastly as the clotted blood they'd evacuated from Ghada's injuries.

"The sandstorm came out of the blue, lasted

long enough only to take the helicopter down. Ghadah was on her way back from her husband's grave in his home town. It's the first time she let Jameelah go with her. It's why she's here, like this, instead of in the emergency compartment, being treated for simple fractures."

Larissa raised horrified eyes to him. "Faress…"

"She wasn't wearing a seat belt," Faress grated, his voice fracturing, agony made sound, for her ears only, even though Ghada was beyond hearing him. "She must have left her seat to wrap her body around Jameelah to protect her. And she did. Jameelah was on the side that sustained the most damage. She would have been killed on impact like the co-pilot. Ghada gave her life for her daughter."

"Oh, God, Faress don't say that. We'll save her…"

"We'll fix her injuries. We *have* fixed them. But don't you see?" His tattered groan broke her control, her resolution not to keep looking at what would undermine her stamina. She looked now at Ghada's monitors, each testimony to a life ebbing by the second. "She's letting go." He raised eyes crimson with fear, drowning in despondency. The cautery probe Larissa was holding crashed to the floor. She barely felt her assistant pushing another into her nerveless hand as Faress's words pummeled her. "She feels what surviving means, that her life as she knows it is over, that she won't be the mother and princess she was and she'd rather die. I know that. I know *her*."

"No, Faress," she sobbed. "She'll live, for Jameelah…for you…for herself…"

Ghada gave her answer to that. She flatlined.

"Defibrillator," Faress roared, had it in his hand charged and ready in seconds, roared again, any resignation scorched away in a blast of terror and determination, "Clear."

The first shock had no effect. Neither did the second. Or third.

And in a fifteen-minute exacerbation of horror, a seizure of desperation, nothing did.

Then there was silence.

Larissa felt as if the very world held its breath, as if time itself had stopped, in recognition not only of such a loss but in awe of the magnitude of grief it inflicted.

Faress stood there, his shocked gaze riveted to his sister's battered form, the shell that no longer housed the woman who'd shared his life from childhood, whom he clearly loved with all of his being.

An eternity later, he moved. Everyone in the compartment lurched out of their paralysis. He reached out and time expanded, magnifying each motion as his hand touched Ghada's lifeless cheek. Gasps of stifled horror spread like wildfire. Then he bent, put his forehead to his sister's, closed his eyes on a shuddering exhalation.

Someone burst out crying. A commotion erupted as others rushed the woman out of Faress's hearing. Not that he seemed to be aware of anything around him. Larissa staggered towards him and the world blinked out. It came back again, to the floor rising up to meet her. At the last moment hands caught her, pulled her up to her feet, but she only saw him, distorted, rippling, through a hot, wet barrier, frozen in the last communion with Ghada, oblivious to everything, a prisoner to the brutality of his unendurable loss.

Suddenly high-pitched bleeps blared, tearing Larissa out of the well of crushing anguish. *Jameelah's monitors.*

Strength and focus surged into her with dizzying suddenness as she exploded to Jameelah's side, met Dr. Tarek's reddened eyes.

"Deepen sedation and regional block," she croaked. "We can't risk general anesthesia."

Tarek nodded, jumping on the reprieve of the need for his skills. Larissa gasped more orders, preparing for the open laparotomy it would take to reach Jameelah's injury and repair it. In a minute she stood poised to start.

She couldn't bear to intrude on Faress's grief, but he was the best surgeon around. She needed him. Jameelah needed him.

"Faress."

At her desperate call he swung up, his empty gaze meeting hers. She meant to say, *I need you.* She couldn't produce a sound, mouthed the entreaty.

He turned his eyes back to Ghada, touched her hand. Larissa saw his lips move, as if he was talking to her. Her heart seized in her chest, but she couldn't afford to give the tragedy one more moment, couldn't wait to see if he'd be able to bring his turmoil under control long enough, well enough to be of any help.

She made the first incision in Jameelah's abdomen, rasped to her first assistant, "Start the cell-saver, get as much blood as you can."

She knew the helicopter's blood bank couldn't have enough blood to cope with the enormous amounts Jameelah would need until they got her hemorrhage under control, not after the amounts they'd used up already. With a cell-saver machine they'd collect, clean and save Jameelah's blood for re-transfusion.

"Cell-saver won't provide a product of good

enough hematocrit value to correct Jameelah's hemorrhagic shock on its own."

Faress. He'd come. Oh, God…

He went on, his face impassive, his voice dead, "Get twenty more units of O-neg."

One of the nurses said, "We have only eight more units."

"I'm O-neg," Larissa said, her voice wavering beyond her control. That made her a universal donor. And though she was pregnant and would usually be unable to donate, she knew there was no risk, when she'd replace what she donated the same day.

Faress's eyes went to her and she thought she saw the Faress she knew, beneath the suffocating layers of unspent suffering, communicating with her, needing her.

Then he turned away. "Lamyaa, see if anyone else is O-neg. Get a blood collection bag for Larissa."

"Make it two," Larissa said. "Just put the volume back into me. I'll get a transfusion as soon as we're back at the complex."

Something like anxiety disturbed the deadness in his eyes. Then he nodded. "Get me two over-the-needle catheters, 18 gauge." Those were in his hands in seconds. He approached her, for the first time since she'd known him depriving her of eye contact. He placed each catheter into the sides of her neck to keep her arms free for the surgery. His technique was so perfect she barely felt the needles piercing her skin.

They found two more O-neg people among them. With two units from each, as well as the cell-saved blood, they'd cover Jameelah's needs.

Without missing a beat, Faress turned to Jameelah, widened the incision Larissa had made, placed self-retaining retractors, until they had maximum visibility and reach. Gritting her teeth against the reality of the little body she was invading, she reached in, pushed the intestines to the side, exposing the aorta for him as their assistants struggled to siphon off a horrifying amount of blood. It took endless minutes before he cross-clamped the aorta, stopping it, only for a feverish race against time to start. All through the procedure her assistant blotted tears instead of sweat.

It took thirty minutes to repair the aortic tear, three times that to explore Jameelah's abdomen for other possible injuries then close her up.

At last Faress took a step back, stared down at Jameelah, for the first time looking at her face. Silence reigned throughout the compartment again. Now the field of surgery had been covered, Jameelah looked like she was sleeping peacefully. Her mother lay dead a dozen feet away. Another wave of empathy and pity crashed through Larissa. This time she let it, no longer trying to slow down the cascade of tears.

The flow became a deluge when Faress bent to his niece, repeated the heart-rupturing gesture of putting his forehead to hers, like he'd done with her mother.

She thought she heard him say, *"La tkhafi, ya sagheerati, ana baadi ma'ek."*

Don't be afraid, my little one. I'm still with you.

The following days were beyond nightmarish.

Only Faress keeping her close made them endurable. Larissa would have gone out of her mind away from him, fearing for his sanity after having Ghada slip through his fingers. She burned with needing to offer support, jumped at the chance to be of use when he delegated to her the task of addressing foreign correspondents, giving his formal statement covering his sister's death. He had enough on his hands, being the surgeon in whose hands she'd died, the crown prince responsible for major public announcements, and the brother who'd had to inform his family of his sister's death.

It had been then she'd had her first sighting of his father and had been shaken to her foundations.

In her line of work she dealt with grieving

parents all the time, had seen people from resigned to manic. But the king's reaction to the news of his daughter's death was horrifying. He was. All her fears of him had multiplied as she'd watched Faress struggle to contain his rage and grief.

Then the first devastating crest passed and Faress still had to deal with the funeral and with a grieving nation. Princess Ghada had been a truly beloved princess and her passing reverberated throughout the kingdom like an earthquake.

All through they shared Jameelah's vigilant follow-up, her constant improvement the only ray of light in the catastrophe. But that was dimmed by the dread of having to face her with the news of her mother's death. Faress decreed it wouldn't be until she was back to full health, trusting no one but himself and Larissa near her when he let her surface from sedation.

Everything settled into pervasive resignation until two weeks to the day they had lost Ghada Faress declared that they'd resume their schedule, that work and other patients waited for no one.

With a battered heart Larissa hoped preoccupation would help him to regain his balance, start to heal his wounds.

That first day back at the complex was like going to Ghada's funeral all over again. Everyone was subdued, and around Faress silent, tense, in respect for his loss and continued suffering.

That night, going back to the palace, Faress held her hand. Larissa tore her eyes away from his profile, berating herself for obsessively watching for any chink in his suffering where she could enter and offer something, anything that might help alleviate even a wisp of it.

She stared at the magnificence of the most advanced city she'd ever seen, one that gave the impression it had all been erected whole that day to the most lavish standards, while constantly evolving with extreme-concept projects that rose between soaring mirrored buildings without disturbing the perfectly realized surroundings. She failed to be impressed tonight. Any pleasure in her surroundings had been extinguished along with Ghada's life. Living with Faress's grief was turning everything into torment instead.

Faress as usual walked her to her guest house. At her door, he took her in a fierce hug that lifted her off her feet, then he abruptly let her go before she could cling, and walked away so fast he seemed to dissolve into the night.

She stood transfixed for endless minutes, swaying, shaking, struggling for breath. And she knew. She had to go after him.

She staggered through the extensive, ingeniously landscaped and lit grounds, her awe rising even now at what permeated them—the entitlement of the all-powerful prince Faress was, the subtlety of the man and the sensitivity of the surgeon. In the distance rose the sprawling stone palace that spoke of all that and everything else that Faress was.

She felt his guards' invisible eyes monitoring her every move, relaying them ahead to forward stations. She wondered if they'd stop her until they asked Faress how to deal with her intruding outside her permitted territory.

They didn't stop her, and when she was on the steps leading to the columned patio, footmen seemed to appear from nowhere, rushed to open the gigantic double doors for her, treating her with all the deference they'd offer Faress himself.

She wobbled into a circular, columned hall that sprawled under a hundred-foot-high stained-glass dome, swayed as the doors were closed soundlessly behind her. Her gaze slammed around but there was no one there to meet her and in her hectic state and the subdued lighting she got only impressions of a sweeping floor extending on both sides, felt a male influence, Faress's, in décor and furnishing, a virile presence, his, permeating the place. Her nervous gaze ended up where thirty-foot-wide marble stairs rose a dozen feet before reaching a spacious platform that extended each side of the upper floor.

Suddenly her gaze dragged to the top of one side and her heart kicked. A shadow detached itself from the depth of darkness, moving soundlessly into the light.

Faress. Haggard and heart-wrenching in the first indigenous garb she'd ever seen him in, a black robe, an *abaya*, trimmed in gold thread. He looked as if he'd stepped out from another world, another time, almost supernatural in mien and impact. But it was the fevered emotions radiating from him that shook her.

She ran up, needing to be near him, stopped a step beneath him, shaking, her tears flowing free, her larynx a fiery coal. "I *hurt* for you…" she wailed. "As much as I hurt for myself when I lost my own sister to a senseless accident, too, just before I came here. She—she was everything to me…"

His nostrils flared, his jaw muscles bunched. Then the rawness that had replaced all emotions in his eyes melted in a flare of empathy.

"Did you have a chance to fight for her?"

She hiccuped a tearing sob at the enormous

emotion thickening his voice. She shook her head, sent tears splashing over her lips, her forearms, the floor.

"Then your loss is even worse, arriving too late, deprived of the chance to try to save her, or to even say goodbye."

"Oh, God, no, Faress, arriving too late was like a single bullet to the heart. Not like the hail that shredded you as Ghada slipped through your fingers. The hope, the dread, the desperation, the crushing responsibility. Oh, God, Faress, the way you suffered, still suffer, I can't bear it!"

Something unbridled detonated in his eyes. She cried out at its impact, reached out trembling hands, offering all that she was, if it would only alleviate a portion of his suffering.

He took her up on her offer, bent and swept her up in his arms. Then the world moved in hard, hurried thuds, each one hitting her with vertigo, the pressure of emotion almost snuffing out her consciousness.

Then she was sinking into a resilient surface, into cool softness, enveloped by his scent, shrouded by dim lights and incense, by virility and craving.

He came down half over her and she moaned with the blow of stimulation, emotional and physical, of her first real contact with him, her first exposure to the full measure of his ferocity, his hunger.

He rose over her, his hands trembling in her confined hair, releasing it, spreading its thickness beneath her, then burying his face in it and breathing her in hard. "I couldn't have survived the past two weeks without you, Larissa, *habibati, hayati, abghaki, ah'tajek…*" Then he took her lips.

He'd called her his love, his life, had told her he wanted her, *needed* her. And if it had been possible to let him take her very life to fill his needs, she would have surrendered it. She surrendered what she could now, all of herself.

He must have felt the totality of her offer, plunged deeper into her mouth until she felt him touching her essence, drawing it into him, his tongue thrusting in furious rhythm, deep and carnal, each plunge riding a growl of insatiability, sending molten agony to her core, carrying on it his dominance, his imperiousness, his surrender and supplication.

Then his hands were everywhere, down her length, fusing her to him, on her buttocks, pressing her against his steely erection, in her elasticated waistband, dragging her T-shirt out then over her head, on her flesh beneath, sending a high-voltage current streaking through her to the rhythm of his feverish stroking before both hands circled her waist, raised her against the headboard, bringing her confined breasts level with his face. Then he buried it there, nuzzled her fiercely.

She cried out with the excess of sensation, with seeing the dark majesty of his head against her bursting flesh. Overcome, she let her hands fulfill the fantasy she'd thought would remain one for ever, burying their hunger in the luxuriance of his mane, pressing his head harder to her.

He rumbled something deep and driven, the sound spearing from his lips directly into her heart. Then he tore himself from her convulsing grip. She cried out as if he'd wrenched her hands off.

Before she could flay herself for being so wanton that she might have appalled him, he spread her on her back again, captured her hands in one of his, stretched her arms above her head. She twisted in mortification, turned her face into sheets laden with his scent, unable to withstand his burning scrutiny.

"Look at me, *ya galbi*." His demand overrode her will and distress, drew her eyes to his. She lurched at the darkness there, the pain. "Let me see you, feel you, your beauty, your vitality…"

And she understood. He needed to feel her life, to counteract the horror of losing someone so loved, so alive, so senselessly.

Needing to offer her body, her very life for his pleasure, his comfort, she arched up, let him undo her bra, expose breasts turgid with pregnancy and arousal.

"Ma ajmallek ya galbi...anti rao'ah..." He closed trembling hands on her breasts and she arched off the bed in a shock of pleasure, making a fuller offering of her flesh. He tore his *abaya* off, half exposing a body chiseled from living granite by virility gods and endless stamina and discipline.

Her awed hands trembled over his perfection. "How beautiful you are... *You* are the wonder..."

He caught her hands again, spread her arms wide at her sides. "Explore me, lay claim to my every inch later, Larissa, later."

He growled as he swooped down on her, rubbed his hair-roughened chest against her breasts until she thrashed beneath him, bucked. Then he bent, opened his mouth over first one breast then the other, as if he'd devour her. Between long, hard draws on each nipple that had her writhing, sobbing, begging, he told her exactly that. That he wanted all of her now. *Now.*

"Bareedek kollek, daheenah, habibati. Daheenah."

She lay powerless under the avalanche of need as her clothes disappeared under his urgency. The spike of ferocity in his eyes at his first sight of her full nakedness should have been alarming. It only sent her heart hurtling with shyness, with pride that her sight affected him that intensely, with the brutality of anticipation. Her moans became keens as he sought her womanhood, his fingers parting her, sliding between her folds, his face contorting on something primal when he felt the heat and moistness of her readiness. She convulsed on the pleasure, hazing with it, with failing to imagine what union with him would bring if a touch unraveled her body and mind. Her stifled cries harmonized with his rumbles, the sound of his steel control snapping.

He came over her and the feel of him, his mass and maleness and power between her legs melted all her heart, all her insides, each thrust at her core through the last barrier of clothes wrenching more pleas from her depths. He rose to both knees to free himself, his lips spilling feverish worship into hers, proclaiming her soul of his heart, raggedly confessing his need to be inside her. *"Roh galbi, mehtaj akoon jow'waki…"*

And she couldn't bear not having him inside her, couldn't bear the emptiness he'd created inside her, couldn't…couldn't…

Oh, God! She *couldn't*.

She went rigid, almost wailed, "Faress, please, *stop*…"

CHAPTER SEVEN

LARISSA felt her plea pummeling Faress.

He lurched and his hand stilled, his lips froze on her neck. Tension buzzed through every muscle imprinted on hers. Then slowly, so slowly, he rose above her, his face taut, his breathing harsh, his eyes unreadable.

He'd be justified to think she'd been leading him on, to even disregard her flimsy demand, give her what her body was screaming for.

But she had no doubt he wouldn't. Faress would never impose himself on her, on any woman. Not even after she'd led him on. But how she wished she could tell him to forget her outburst, to just take her, now.

But she couldn't let him take her, share ultimate intimacies with her, not under false pretenses. And it would be just that with him still ignorant of the truth. He probably wouldn't want to come near her when he finally learned it.

But how could she tell him now? Ghada's death had nearly destroyed him. How could she tell him that he'd lost his brother too? The brother he kept talking about with such love and longing? Jawad's death had been over two months ago, but to him it would happen the moment he learned of it. She couldn't inflict another beloved sibling's death on him now.

She could only do one thing. Beg his forgiveness.

She didn't hope she'd obtain it. She'd given him the first reason to think the worst of her. And just thinking she'd lose his good opinion brought on again the tears that had dried in the heat of her hunger.

"Faress, please, forgive me, I needed to be with you, b-but I—I..." And she could say no more.

Faress raised himself on arms so stiff they wouldn't have felt more painful with an infarction. But the agony was the urge to fill their emptiness with her beloved body.

He filled his sight and senses, his memory, with her instead as she lay spread beneath him, beyond his fantasies, lush and vital and all female, his female, aflame in the dark solitude of his bed, exposed and vulnerable and the most overwhelming power he'd ever known. Her power over him was absolute. And she was cradling him in the only place he'd ever call home, the moist heat of her welcome unraveling his sanity.

But what was shriveling his heart was the sight of her tears, tears of distress again, the pummeling memory of what she'd come here confessing, sharing. Her similar, mutilating loss. The loss he would have given anything to discover, to heal. And what had he done when she'd finally worked up the fortitude to talk about it, if only under the pressure of catastrophic circumstances and the need to offer *him* solace? He'd swept her to his bed.

And she'd begged *his* forgiveness. *Ya Ullah.*

He should be the one on his knees, asking hers. If she hadn't asked him to stop, he would have been lost inside her now, minutes away from release. And it didn't matter that he knew he would have given her the same pleasure. What mattered was that he'd snatched at her the moment she'd offered herself, rushed her seduction, short-changed her cherishing, would have turned their long-craved, their *sacred* first time together into a frenzied mating. The first time she hadn't even been here offering.

He carefully lifted his body from the cradle of hers, shuddered at the sensations even severing contact with her detonated inside him. But mostly at feeling the same brutal desire eating through her, wrenching at his, clamping his loins in agony, such a contrast with the agitation shaking her all over and the shyness spreading peach through her cream.

And he knew. What he now realized he'd known all along but had never dwelt on. What everything about her, every word and look and tremor since they'd met had been telling him.

She was a virgin. He was certain. No man had ever plundered her pleasures.

Alhamdolel'Lah… Thank God she'd stopped him. The crime of rushing not only their first time but hers would have been irretrievable.

But she *had* stopped him. And now he couldn't stop pride from surging in guilt's wake. Though her sexual experience hadn't even been an issue with him before, though he liked to think he'd left the elemental possessiveness of his heritage behind, now he knew she had none, he couldn't help the rush of exultation that his mate would know no other man's touch.

But if, without experience, she'd responded to him, enslaved his senses this way, he couldn't even imagine what it would be like, what she'd do to him once he initiated her into the rites of passion, swept her into the abandoned realms of sensual decadence, once she applied all that genius and skill to becoming a mistress of the arts of pleasure as she was in the arts of healing.

But it wasn't time to torment himself with those projections. It was enough now that he knew. He'd be her first. And her only.

Only not now. Only when he could offer her all of himself untainted by grief, by any form of emotional dilution. It had to be soon. It would be.

He swung his legs to the floor, reached for the cover he'd tossed aside in preparation for entering the bed that had been a barren desert strewn with thorns until she'd come, the bed he needed her to never leave. He turned back to her, started to slide the cover over her, feet, then legs, going up, hearing the whisper of rich cotton gliding over richer velvet skin, savoring her every jerk, every moan betraying her enjoyment, her torment. When he reached her waist, he gave in, took more suckles of the breasts that had re-whetted his appetite for life. The music of her gasps, the intoxication of her squirming, the hands that, in spite of her intentions, clamped his head to her engorged-with-need flesh, begging his devouring, and the scent of her arousal sent blood crashing in his head, thundering in his loins.

It took all his will to end his feast of her, tuck the cover beneath her armpits, covering up her temptation. Then he dropped kisses across one shoulder, up her neck to her lips then down the other side. Her trembling was constant by the time he withdrew.

He soothed her, smoothed his hand over the luxury of her incredible tresses. "It's me who begs your forgiveness, *ya rohi*. You came here so magnanimously offering me haven from my turmoil and I took your offer where you didn't mean it to go. Not yet. And justifiably so. When I take you, not one second of my possession of you, my pleasuring of you will be tainted by any need but my need for every inch of you, every quiver, every cry, every satisfaction. I won't take you when the need for solace in your arms is an ingredient that mars the purity, the ferocity of my need for you."

A strangled sound escaped her, and he swooped to take it into him, opening his lips over hers.

"I admit," he muttered between deep, then deeper plunges into the maddening fount of her taste, "Though it's an impossibility not to be aroused to the point of pain at the mere thought of you, my need for your haven is as great now." He withdrew to fill his sight with her, her beauty ripened with need for him, to make his urgent request. "Will you bestow it on me?"

Her tears flowed heavier as she held out shaking arms to him. On a groan of sweetest relief and triumph, he filled them, came down beside her. He turned her to her side, plastered his chest to her naked back, then wrapped himself all around her, filled his aching limbs with her preciousness, settled into another form of intimacy to what his body was roaring for.

And if he'd needed proof of how much he loved her, this was it. Just holding her permeated him with the peace he'd thought he'd never experience again, with a feeling of invincibility, brought him far more pleasure than all his life's previous intimacies combined. But, then, she *was* his life's first true intimacy.

Larissa had been awake for a few minutes. She kept her eyes closed.

She didn't want the sight of her surroundings to distract her from savoring the memories of her life's most incredible night.

Faress had not only not been angry at her contradictory behavior, he'd left her in awe of his control again, in agony at his trust, exonerating her, even apologizing for almost taking what she'd offered so fully.

Then he'd bestowed another privilege on her, letting her offer him solace. For hours she'd lain awake, scared of wasting one second of experiencing him, listening to his every breath, her heart vibrating to his every heartbeat as he'd lain awake too, fully aroused yet drenching her with tenderness. It had been beyond any intimacy lovemaking could have imparted, a sharing of such profundity she hadn't known two separate beings could share.

She didn't know when sleep had claimed her, but it was clear it had, and it had been her life's most peaceful and rejuvenating.

She lay savoring the imprint of his every inch on hers even now he wasn't there, finally knowing one thing.

Everything would work out. She just knew that when she judged it possible to burden him with the truth, he'd understand why she'd withheld it, would let her be there for him in yet another loss and everything would eventually end up resolved for the best.

She opened her eyes. Only because the need to see him again had built to an unmanageable level. And because she had to get ready, get *dressed* before he came back.

She jumped out of bed, *his* bed, ran across the gigantic, almost spartan room, snatched the clothes he'd folded with care on the back of an armchair by a matching desk with just a laptop on it and streaked to the door she hoped was the bathroom.

It was. The most incredible place she'd ever been. An honest-to-goodness *hammam*, his own Turkish bath. Three interconnected halls, with the middle one she'd just entered ringed by arches supported by a dozen tapering columns, sprawling beneath a soaring dome with stained-glass windows that created an otherworldly half-light. Below the dome was a raised marble platform of purest white that seemed to glow in the unearthly illumination. This had to be the hot room, the equivalent of a sauna.

Images invaded her mind, her nerve endings, of Faress, naked, lying face down on the marble as steam swirled around his magnificent body, his muscles glistening, their tautness after their exhausting days relaxing under her hands as she rubbed him down, hands and lips lost in tactile nirvana as she tasted him, tongue and teeth overdosing on virility made flesh. Then he turned to her, yanked her to him, plastered her to his slick, heated flesh, let her feel what she'd done to him before laying her down on the marble, spreading her, coming over her…

Sounds outside jerked her out of her erotic haze. He might have returned! And she was standing here in his bathroom, naked and almost reverting to a fluid state with hunger for him.

With the breath knocked out of her she rushed in search of a shower cubicle, found it, turned on perfect-temperature water, stepped inside, her blood tumbling with arousal at the elaborate images her mind generated, of sharing this place's pleasures with Faress. Suddenly her blood congealed as the images turned vicious, showing him sharing it with other women, maybe many at once…

No, *no*. He wasn't like that.

But even if he were, who was she to presume to judge him? He treated her with all the chivalry of a knight of the desert, the elevation of a born prince, but he only wanted her for a lover, would never want her for more. Wouldn't want her at all when he learned the truth. She had no claim on him. Would never have any. Even if his claim on her was for life and beyond and… Oh—oh…

Oh, God.

She should have known. What had been happening to her since she'd laid eyes on him. It wasn't only that he'd bowled her over and she wanted him like she'd never known she could want. It wasn't only that his company had been what had kept her sanity together, what had suppressed her grief and fear of the future. It wasn't only that she'd counted on his collaboration and advice to center her, to extract from her a level of efficiency she hadn't known she was capable of. It wasn't only that she'd gotten so dependent on his support she knew she'd feel its loss like a crippling physical one.

That was all true and had been horrible enough.

But the truth was far more so.

She loved him.

All the way to no return, with everything in her.

Knowing herself, she should have realized her unprecedented reaction to him *had* been love at first sight.

But she'd never believed it could ever happen to her. Though, heaven knew, she should have. Hadn't Claire fallen in love with Jawad the same way? Hadn't that love turned out to be not only real but the only absolute reality in her life? The one thing that had overpowered her love of everything and everyone, her love of life itself? Hadn't it been the reason she'd died?

And she was so like Claire. Why had she believed she'd be different in that?

She should have run away after those first days, before his spell had become total, unbreakable. She should have found some other way to solve her dilemma.

But she hadn't. She'd stayed, greedy for more of anything with him, drowning in him. And though he wanted her, had last night lavished loving endearments on her, she knew they had been nothing more than what the passionate man he was had lavished on the woman he'd craved in the heat of lust. She couldn't dream her overriding feelings for him could be reciprocated. He was beyond such hopes.

She laid her forehead on the cool marble wall, suffocating with yet another head-on crash with merciless reality.

She'd lost everything loving him, any chance of happiness or even peace. She'd never have anyone else in her life, let alone love again. But she would have realized that sooner or later. Realizing that now made no difference.

And then none of this had been about her in the first place.

This was all about Claire's and Jawad's baby.

And if she told Faress, assured the baby's future, and Faress still wanted her, she'd take anything he offered, for as long as he offered it. She only hoped he wouldn't be too angry with her, cut her off, or at least opt out of any liaison with her in fear of complicating his relationship with someone he'd have in his life through his brother's baby. She hoped he'd realize that when he chose to end it, she'd bow out, never cause him any discomfort.

Drawing in painful breaths, she reached for a bar of rich white soap and began lathering his loofah with it, trying to bring her tumultuous emotions under control.

She failed. Everything here smelt of him, felt like him, each whiff, each vibe sending her into spiraling misery and sensory overload. *Just get out of here…*

She stumbled through a slapdash shower, was dressed and desperately gulping steadying breaths in under five minutes.

She heard nothing outside, had probably imagined hearing the noises before. But now she *felt* him outside.

She tried to school her features, her emotions. She'd rush out and throw herself in his arms if she didn't get those under control.

With one last inhalation, she stepped out. Knowing she was fighting a losing battle, that her feelings must be emblazoned all over her face, she walked towards him as he stood by the desk, indescribable in tight-fitting black pants and white shirt, looking down in absorption at an open file. Her heart ricocheted in her chest in anticipation of seeing new levels of intimacy, no matter how superficial and transient in his eyes after last night.

At her approach, he turned.

Her heart stopped. Then it almost burst.

This wasn't Faress. This was a stranger.

An incensed stranger looking at her out of his eyes.

She groped for the armchair's support, swayed, her eyes prisoner to the rage in his, her soul burning with it.

She'd left it too late. She'd lost her chance to be the one to tell him the truth.

He'd somehow found out.

Faress stared at Larissa, rage and disillusion consuming him.

The woman he'd fallen in love with, the *only* woman he'd ever fallen in love with, laid his heart in her hands, at her feet.

A liar. A manipulator. A merciless cheat.

He'd found out just an hour ago. As she'd slept in his bed in the aftermath of what he'd believed to be his life's first true intimacy. He'd left her side unquestioning that he'd found the other half of his soul, that she'd saved his sanity by her empathy and magnanimity. He'd intended to come back to her with his mother's betrothal anklet, kneel at her feet and offer his heart and honor, his life and beyond.

He had it in his pocket now, felt as if each priceless stone studding it was a prism focusing his agony into an unerring laser targeting his heart, shriveling it, his reason, charring it.

But what almost sent him over the brink was the destruction of his last hope. He *had* been clinging to it, even in the face of all evidence. He *had* been hoping he'd face her with his fury and disillusion only to see her innocence in her eyes, in confusion and hurt. But what he saw there was her realization that he'd found her out, her admission that her crimes were grave enough to warrant any punishment.

He saw *fear* in her eyes for the first time. And he knew.

The woman he loved with everything in him had never existed.

So that was why she'd never told him more… *anything* about herself. *Ya Ullah,* how had he never grown suspicious when she'd steered him so masterfully away from anything that could give him clues about her life?

"Faress…" His name on her lips quaked through him. Still. He gritted his teeth against her siren's song, made overpowering now with the imploring quaver braiding through it. "Please…let me…"

He turned on her, crimson blotching his sight, black eclipsing his heart and reason. "Let you what? Lie to me some more?" At her gasp, the way she squeezed her eyes as if against a mortal blow, he lost it. "Let *me*," he bellowed, feeling the shards of his shattered heart shredding his ribcage, "spare you the effort of coming up with more lies. Which were never lies, of course, just omissions of the truth. Isn't that what you wanted to say? Now, do you want to know how luck betrayed you? When you could…*would* have gotten away with it for ever? It was because Ghada died."

The tears filling her stricken eyes spilled at hearing Ghada's name, splashing down her velvet cheeks. Everything in him roared with the need to reach for her, comfort her, ward off the pain he was inflicting. Then a lacerating voice lashed him.

You're inflicting nothing. Anything you see or feel from her now is part of the ongoing pretense.

He went mad with pain. "It was only because she died that I broke my promise to Jawad. You know, the insane pledge he made me take? What made you so sure I would never tie you to him?"

"Faress, no, please," she sobbed. "I didn't—"

"Didn't know that he made me pledge to never look for him?" he cut her off, his voice shearing, terrible, unrecognizable. "That he'd contact me only on condition that I remained ignorant of his whereabouts, his life? You want me to believe you didn't know he renounced our ways and his family, abdicated his birthright, hid from us for the last eight years? You let me talk and talk about him and all the time *you knew*."

She nodded, her lips trembling so hard they constantly escaped her teeth's efforts to still them. Acknowledging the truth of his words, or only his right to believe them under the circumstances? If the latter, *was* there another explanation…?

Ya Ullah, he still believed there'd be extenuating circumstances? That she'd turn out not to be the fraud the facts revealed her to be?

Incensed further by his inability to overcome her spell, he ground out, his voice butchered, the howl of a mortally wounded beast, "Too bad for you I broke my pledge. Because Ghada died and I thought he should know. Because even though you made me believe I could share my loss with you, she still wasn't a part of you. Because she was a part of *him* and I needed him to share *her* loss."

At this Larissa's silent tears spiked on a hot, sharp lament, a lance penetrating his heart with the force of a heart attack.

He ignored the agony, hurtled on, "Too bad for you I needed him, needed my older brother. So I searched for him. And an hour ago, I got this."

He slammed his open palm down on the file that had taken his one remaining sibling from him, just as it ended all his hopes and pulverized his heart. The desk splintered under his agonized fury.

Larissa was weeping openly now, the sight of her desolation, her false, self-serving desolation skewering through his skull with another wave of rage and misery.

"He hid so well in the new land he'd made his home, even my intelligence service got hazy information on his life there. He was so afraid that if anyone knew where he was, our father would too, and he would tear him away or, worse, poison his life there, end his happiness, even harm his beloved. He even feared telling me. *Me.*" And he'd go insane with regret, with guilt, for the rest of his life that he hadn't overridden that fear, disregarded it and *made* Jawad share his self-made privileges. Now it was too late. Too late. He roared with it all. "And just when I did what I should have done years ago, found him, I learned that he died in his self-imposed exile, sick and alone." Larissa shook her head, hiccuped, one hand extending to quake its negation. "You're trying to say he wasn't alone? That he had a loving wife at his side? Yes, I had an indistinct photo of his wife. A woman with flaming red hair and a willowy body. *You.*"

She staggered, collapsed where she stood with the wrath of his last shout, ended up on the floor, clinging to the chair he'd kept between them so he wouldn't reach for her, touch her and lose what remained of his mind and control. He was close enough with her looking up at him with those miraculous eyes wild with shock.

Why shock? Why now? And he even assumed this could be real? From the woman who'd lied so seamlessly, whose very vibes had sworn to him of her inexperience in the ways of the flesh? When she'd been his brother's for eight years? In a marriage that, from the little Jawad had told him of the woman he'd left the whole world for, had been blazingly sensual? And it had remained so till the day he'd died. Otherwise Jawad would have come back to them.

The woman he worshipped body and soul was the same woman Jawad had worshipped the same way…inconceivable, unendurable…

He went down on his haunches. Unable to stand any more. Unable to stand seeing her at his feet this way when he should relish it. He didn't, felt every nerve punishing him with the need to haul her up, carry her to the bed they'd shared all night, turn back the clock, wipe his memory clean.

He flayed his stamina for a minute, watching her

tears, imagining them changing color in her distress.

Then he groaned, "*B'Ellahi,* why did you come here?"

She shuddered, wiped a trembling hand over her wet lips, started to open them. Did she think he wanted an answer? Could bear listening to her adding to the lies?

"I'll tell you why," he grated across her first wavering syllable. "You came here intent on getting the wealth and privileges you married Jawad for. You must have been enraged when they never materialized, when Jawad threw away all he was born into in his pursuit of your love and a so-called normal life with you. You must have lasted that long with him only in hope you'd one day get an unimaginable return on your investment of years of putting up with his infatuation and acting the part of the devoted wife and lover—a life as a queen."

She kept shaking her head, jerking with each word soaked with the venom of his agony as if with the lash of a whip, her tears splashing his hands, wetting the hardwood floor.

Her distress corroded him as if it were real. But it could only be the distress of a criminal caught in the act and fearing retribution, or at least the loss of her projected gains. After the unparalleled effort she'd put into her flawless charade, too. Appealing to him on every level, projecting the illusion of the soulmate who instinctively knew him down to his last impulse and thought, who shared his views and goals, who understood and appreciated him like he'd never been, would never be, understood or appreciated…

Ya Ullah… How could he live with the loss of all that?

Losing both his siblings was more endurable. He retained so much of them, their love and their integrity, his love for them, faith in them, memories of them.

But with Larissa he'd lost everything. He'd been stripped of all he'd had before he'd known her. She might have lost a gamble, a highest-stakes one, but she'd cost him everything worth having.

Feeling the deadness of resignation invading his being, he welcomed it, hurried it on as he rasped, "So when Jawad died without giving you what you wanted, you went for plan B. With his extensive knowledge of me at your disposal, you came here armed with all you needed to lay your trap, aiming to capture another Aal Rusheed brother, this time one in his full power, one capable of handing you the world. Too bad for you that you failed."

* * *

Each word of rage, of pain, each look of disillusion and disgust had been a knife twisting in Larissa's vitals. But that summation, that verdict was a mortal blow she couldn't survive.

She had to ward it off, fought the muteness, choked out her only defense, the truth. *"I only came here for the baby."*

At the word "baby" Faress staggered up and backwards as if blown away by the force of a detonation, only the collision with the now-askew desk aborting his momentum. He looked at her with the same shocked eyes that had acknowledged Ghada's death. Worse, with the eyes of someone looking at the woman who'd just shot him in the heart.

After a mutilating stretch of harsh-breathing, bone-quaking silence he finally rasped in a voice that felt no longer like sound, but like pain, like bleeding, "You have a baby?"

She'd already blurted it out, but to have to elaborate on it, detail the specifics, when he looked down at her that way…

Another geyser of tears flowed out of her eyes. "N-no…I'm—I'm pregnant…f-fourteen weeks n-now…" Then she broke down.

It could have been an hour while Faress stood frozen, looking down at her as if at an impossibility, a monstrosity, while she surrendered to the crushing breakers of misery.

When they finally receded enough, after they'd made sure she was within a breath of unconsciousness, she had to state another part of the truth. For the record. She had no hope for amnesty.

"I thought Jawad was an orphan. I—I only found out who he really was after he died. And when I came here and met you, I had no idea who you were until I saw that magazine..."

She choked on another wave of desolation, fell silent.

At length, he talked, his voice a dead monotone, "So you came here, signed up for this job, and didn't know I was the current crown prince, and your boss?"

She raised her gaze to him, hoping to find a glimpse of the Faress she knew. There wasn't. He was gone. She still had to make this stranger understand how things had developed.

She forced in a trembling inhalation. "Jawad and Claire died within a week of each other and the weeks afterwards... they were a nightmare. I was pregnant and suddenly alone and I had to rearrange my life around having the baby with no help and with a job like mine. I was desperately looking for alternative career paths when I discovered the baby did have a family. But I couldn't contact you, I thought it might be a mistake. I—I haven't heard good things a-about your father, and your family *was* the family Jawad had cut all relations with. But since I didn't know what drove him away I thought I'd try to find out for myself if it had been something serious because I owed it to the baby to try to give him a family. I took this job knowing only that it was in Bidalya where I could gather information about your family before deciding whether to approach you or not. And then I met you and it all spun out of control. But I did it all for the baby. And I-I'm still not sure if it would be in his best interests to have the Aal Rusheeds for a family…"

"His?" he interrupted, his eyes obsidian chips of steel. "You talk as if you think it's a boy."

"I—I know it is," she stammered. "I had a maternal blood test. Jawad wanted to know." A memory detonated, of Jawad's face as he'd made that demand, drained, emaciated but laughing, excited. "He had a relapse…leukemia, and after the treatment cycle had an infection. He was sure he'd beat it, like he had so many times before, so he wanted to know which gender to shop for the minute he was out of hospital, which he estimated to be by the time the test became possible. But he never made it out… He—he died the very next day."

Something horrifying scraped from the depths of Faress's chest as he dropped into the chair, the sound of his brother's death congealing into reality, another scar gouged in his psyche.

She fought off the horror, the need to rise and throw her arms around him, rid him of all his agony, his rage, at whatever cost to her. She choked on instead, "I still had the test at six weeks, felt as if he'd know w-when I did…"

Faress exploded to his feet, his eyes crazed with pain and rage beyond control. "What a poignant tale," he snarled, vicious, almost inhuman. "What a perfect angel."

Her heart nearly burst out of her ribs. Oh, *God*…

She shouldn't have told him about the baby, should have left Bidalya with her secret intact!

His fury, his contempt were so annihilating, they might reach explosive levels if she tried to defend herself any further.

Her only consolation was that she hadn't told him the whole truth. And as long as he believed she was Jawad's widow, she had some power. He wouldn't think any better of her if he learned she wasn't. His accusation would still stand. The sister of Jawad's widow could as easily aspire to be a queen, using the privileged information gleaned from Jawad about him as an entrapping weapon. If she confessed now, he'd only know she had less claim to the baby than he thought, and would most likely snatch him away the moment he was born.

If he did, the baby would be the king's to raise, and she'd seen the evidence of the king's brand of upbringing in Jawad. Even if he had been the most loving, sensitive man on earth, he'd suffered deep grief, had been scarred, and she now knew it had been his father who'd scarred him.

Faress had survived his father unscathed, but he was infinitely stronger than Jawad, than anyone she'd ever known. And then, being the younger son, the king probably hadn't focused on him. Also, from what she'd heard, Faress's mother had been a powerful woman who'd kept the king in check before Faress. She'd probably been the buffer who'd kept Faress and Ghada from their father's influence. But she hadn't been able to protect her firstborn, his heir, whom he'd pressured and twisted to his heart's content.

But the baby, if Faress took him away, would have no mother to fight for him. And no matter how loving Faress was, as she'd seen him with Jameelah, he was simply too busy to take a real part in the baby's upbringing. He would be at the mercy of an unreasonable old man, have no more maternal care than the indifferent service of distant female relatives and servants.

She couldn't let that happen. No matter what the cost. To her.

"So…no more fabrications?" She jerked at Faress's rumble, that of a lion about to pounce. "No more rewriting of history to make yourself into the selfless, steadfast heroine you've been playing so far? You stand by your story that you didn't come here to get what you wanted all along from Jawad from me?"

She swallowed past the jagged rock that had replaced her larynx, tried to no avail to slow down the flow of tears. She knew they were incensing him further.

"I have no way to prove to you I didn't know anything about you," she whispered. "But even if you think I did, how could I have predicted your reaction when you saw me?"

"Because you had trapped one Aal Rusheed brother before," he growled. "You had him sell out his world, his soul for you. You thought you'd have the same effect on his brother. And I'm sure if it hasn't worked out that way, you had a back-up plan."

His contempt, after she'd had his respect, his trust, pulped her, left her helpless. She tried one last time for the least exoneration, a drowning woman's grab at a straw.

"Your anger, your suspicion," she rasped, "are the result of my actions. But none of them was premeditated. It's been like living on a roller-coaster since we met and most of the time I haven't known if I was coming or going. I couldn't tell you at first for the reasons I told you, because I had no idea what kind of man you were. But the better I knew you, the longer I put it off, the harder it got. I was…*am* still afraid of your father, and I was more afraid every day of your reaction…*this* reaction, and I kept sinking deeper into unintentional deception. But I was going to tell you, come what may, just before Ghada's accident. Then I couldn't tell you, couldn't inflict another sibling's loss on you."

He stared down at her for so long she had a crazy hope he might actually be lost in thought, considering her words.

Then he spoke, and her world came to an end.

"I should be in your debt for such solicitude," he drawled, his voice cold, pitiless, far more devastating than the earlier volcanic emotions. "But I'm so ungrateful I choose not to believe a word you said, or will ever say. You have lied about *everything* so far. You're lying now. With Jawad ill with a disease whose treatment would have damaged his fertility, what are the odds that the child you're carrying is his? Whatever they are, I don't care either way. Right now I care about one thing. That you get out of here. I never want to see you again."

CHAPTER EIGHT

THE flight attendant gave Larissa a pained attempt at a smile as she told her to fasten her seat belt.

Larissa couldn't blame her. A blurred look in the mirror on her way out of Faress's guest house had shown her a blotched, swollen zombie. She'd cried all through the sixteen hours it had taken to organize her departure from Bidalya. She might still be crying now. She was too numb to tell.

After Faress had left her in a heap on his bedroom floor, she'd stumbled back to the guest house somehow, phoned the airport and booked the first flight home. She'd left everything but her passport and credit card behind, had left at once and spent the hours till her flight slumped in a seat against a wall in the furthest corner of Az-Zufranah's airport.

She'd spent every minute telling herself it was for the best for the baby. That Faress, by not believing her and kicking her out of Bidalya, had made for her the decision she'd been agonizing over. That this assured the baby would be safe from his grandfather. She'd tried to tell herself she'd done what she could, that no matter how differently she might have handled this it would have all ended the same way. She'd now be the baby's whole family, should be satisfied she'd tried to give him a family, even if she'd failed. Even if she'd damaged herself irrevocably while doing so…

I never want to see you again.

Faress's icy, final decree had felt like a death sentence. A fatal blow. But she had to live. At least to exist. For the baby.

A fresh wave of desolation rolled through her. She tossed in her seat, the seat belt against her now-larger stomach constricting. She reached uncoordinated hands to loosen it and it struck her.

Something was wrong here. Their first layover was in London. Seven hours from Az-Zufranah. Though she'd been lost in a timeless zone of misery, it couldn't have been that long since take-off. So why had the flight attendant asked her to fasten her seat belt again?

She waited until the woman walked briskly by her seat and called out to her, "Excuse me…why are we fastening our seat belts?"

The exquisite Bidalyan flashed her a wary smile,

as if she was afraid Larissa would start bawling all over her. "We've been recalled to Az-Zufranah airport. The pilot already announced it."

Larissa now remembered hearing the pilot's nasal droning in a few languages. She hadn't caught one word of any. "Recalled? Why?"

The woman shrugged. "Crown Prince Faress's orders."

Larissa gasped. The brunette excused herself and rushed away in alarm, leaving Larissa to struggle with another debilitating surge of agitation. He'd recalled the plane. Why?

She couldn't even imagine his intentions. Any projection carried hope. Hope was far more mutilating now. Despair was at least unambiguous, final, certain.

But hope had a way of springing up where it shouldn't. Of taking hold on non-existent foundations. And for the next half-hour, until they landed, it took her on a ride into yet another brand-new hell.

She sat in her seat, frozen, hypersensitive, until a ripple of gasps and exclamations spread from the business-class section.

She lurched into the aisle, investigating the source of disturbance. And there he was.

Faress.

He saw her at once, too.

With unfathomable eyes fixing on her, he strode towards her, regal in step and dress, towering, beyond description, like an avenging angel, all in white, from the flowing ankle-length *tobe* to the gold-trimmed *abaya* covering it, to the *ghotrah* headdress to even the usually black *eggal* keeping that in place. His bronze skin glowed against all the pristine whiteness, incandescent even in the atrocious cabin lighting.

It hurt, on every level, seeing his beauty, feeling his uniqueness, knowing what she'd lost, what she'd never have.

It was a good thing she was drained or she would have bawled at the sight of him, like the flight attendant had been afraid she would.

He stopped a foot away. Then, in silence, he extended a hand to her. Her eyes gushed. So she wasn't drained after all.

Or tears and misery were simply unending…

Faress sat on his eastern terrace facing a subdued Larissa across the table laid with their elaborate, untouched breakfast.

He'd been trying to keep his eyes off her ravaged beauty, off the uneven rise and fall of her ripe breasts below yet another shapeless outfit, off the glossy fire-fall around her strong, now defenseless shoulders where the cool dawn breeze was combing its invisible fingers, making *his* fingers itch to replace them. He'd been trying to find distraction in the vista that usually imbued him with peace, the magnificent daybreak desert that spread into the horizon after the oasis of his palace grounds ended.

He found no distraction, no peace now. He knew he'd never find them again. Not without her.

He was still reeling. Too many losses, too brutal, too overwhelming, paralyzed him, mind and soul. But after the first tidal wave of discovery, of agony and jealousy and disillusion had devastated him, after suspicion and betrayal had shattered his reason and control, painted everything in ugliness and sordidness, starting with her, it had started to recede.

He'd found himself at her guest house, needing to look into her eyes once more, needing to find closure. At her door he'd known what he'd been there for. Just to find *her* again. And with her the only possible continuation of his life.

What he'd found had been everything she'd brought to Bidalya. Everything she'd left behind.

She hadn't hung around, like the woman capable of such an elaborate charade as he'd accused her of perpetrating would have done. That woman would have known such rage as he'd shown indicated an involvement of surpassing magnitude. A fatal weakness to be exploited, forged in time into unconditional surrender, one he would have been all too eager to offer, to atone for all the malice that had spilled from his lips.

But she hadn't waited to strike while he was at his most unstable, most vulnerable. She'd left. She'd used the hours during which he'd ridden into the desert, when a blanket order not to be disturbed had blocked reports of her departure.

He could have considered her leaving at once, leaving her belongings behind, to be further manipulation. One guaranteeing him to panic, pursue her with carte blanche offers. He hadn't. He'd seen something die inside her at the finality of his contempt, his rejection. Many things had died inside him lately. He'd forever recognize the inimitable loss in others now. He'd recognized it in her. She'd left, never to return.

So he'd given the order ensuring her return then had lain in her unmade bed, to breathe what would make air breathable again—her scent. It had permeated him, bringing back their night in his bed, eclipsing the following fateful morning. And all his pain and jealousy and disillusion had started to fade. And he'd realized.

He didn't care. Why she'd come here or whose

baby she was carrying. She had made him hers, and her baby was as precious to him as his own just because it was hers. Whatever the truth was, there *had* been extenuating circumstances, overwhelming enough to force her into the secrecy she'd maintained and the lies she'd told.

Then as the peace just her memory brought defused more of his upheaval, he surrendered to her echoes around him, to her essence embedded inside him, psyche and soul. He relived their weeks together, the ordeals, the collaboration, the companionship, the breathless anticipation, the boundless hunger, the unadulterated pleasure, the full, absolute *life* of each moment in her company.

And he knew. He knew *her*, from that first moment.

She had hidden the truth, but she hadn't lied.

But having his faith restored in her had only made it worse.

He would have given both arms for her to have been lying, to have been anybody else's. But she'd belonged to Jawad…!

He'd worshipped Jawad, had been gutted over his estrangement, was now devastated over his death. How could he still covet Larissa, knowing she'd been his brother's woman, was now the mother of his unborn child?

And what about her? Before yesterday he'd been certain her emotions had mirrored his. But now he knew what he did, could she have possibly switched from loving Jawad, *mourning* him—which must be a major part of her grief, mixed with her anguish over her sister—to loving *him*? Could he *want* her to, so fast? If she had, what did that say about the depth of her emotions?

He had believed the overriding magic that had enslaved him had enslaved her as quickly, as fully. But what if she was just fickle? Worse, what if he was deluding himself so he could hang onto her and the baby, the last thing he had of his brother?

But if she wasn't the woman he believed her to be, *was* the baby his brother's? That could be proved easily enough, but just the thought of seeking proof made him soul-sick. But, then, he'd already acknowledged he didn't care, that it was enough it was *her* baby. Still, the idea that she might be lying about something so vital, the ramifications…

Her soft inhalation brought him out of his turmoil, caressed his insides, scraped his every nerve ending.

"Faress, I need to tell you…"

He raised his hand, aborting her overture. They'd parted on his vicious words. The first words to be uttered now also had to be his. They might be a grave mistake, but he could do nothing but obey his heart's conviction, risk them.

He inhaled. "It's I who needs to tell you that I went mad with grief and shock yesterday. I now do believe you are carrying Jawad's baby. As a doctor you must have been fully aware of the effects of chemo and radiation therapy on his fertility and you must have frozen sperm beforehand. You got pregnant via IVF?"

She only nodded. He was silent for a moment, fighting back the welling of scorching regret that Jawad hadn't lived long enough to see the baby he'd craved.

He exhaled, resigned by now to the sick electricity arcing through him. "You didn't handle the situation well, but you do have legitimate grounds for your fears, so that makes the course you chose somewhat justifiable. I hope you'll forgive my accusations."

"Oh, God, Faress, it's me who…"

He raised his hand again. He had to get this out in one go. He kept his eyes fixed on a point in the horizon behind her. "I've given the situation a lot of thought. I've found only one solution. You must marry me."

Faress felt the dry proposal, the imperious

command gash him on its way out. This wasn't how he'd dreamt of offering himself to her. But everything had changed. For now he had to claim her and Jawad's child as his own, protect them, offer them all the privileges that should have been Jawad's if not for their father's injustice. Larissa had come here looking for her baby's heritage and family. This would be the immediate reason she'd accept his proposal. Then when one day they both managed to bury Jawad, they could let their emotions surface past the grief and the guilt…

He gritted his teeth against the surge of desire and desolation. *Ya Ullah*, would he ever be able to forget? Would she?

He forced his eyes back to her to read her reaction. What he saw threatened his sanity. It was beyond endurance, watching the precarious control she'd been maintaining over herself coming undone, seeing her in the grip of such profound heartbreak.

Was this her grief over Jawad surfacing in full measure at last? Was she desolate over loving *him*, consumed by guilt for letting go of Jawad so soon? Or was it because she only wanted him, when her heart and soul belonged with Jawad still, the guilt far more lacerating for him being Jawad's brother?

Desperate to ameliorate her anguish, to lessen

the emotional impact, the intimate implications of his proposal, he rasped, "I wouldn't have proposed this now if you weren't pregnant. And I am destined to marry for duty anyway, to produce heirs. And you've already proved fertile…"

Her weeping only got worse. He measured the magnitude of his stamina. It was three minutes of watching Larissa dissolve in misery. Then it snapped.

"I presume these aren't tears of relief?" he grated. She shook her head on another ragged sob. "You mean you refuse?" She nodded, her sobs slowing, as if she was running out of power.

He stared at her bent head, relief washing over him. She was still committed to Jawad, wasn't inconstant, as he'd feared.

Next moment a new surge of rage and devastation crashed on him.

If her refusal was final, that meant she didn't want him at all. So what had the past weeks meant? She'd said no to his advances at first, but every look and breath and word since had only been saying not yet. So had her desire been faked? And if so, why? She still loved Jawad, had only wanted what was rightfully hers and her baby's, then she'd stumbled on him and thought if he was smitten enough, he'd give her what the Aal

Rusheeds owed them? But she didn't want it if he was included in the bargain?

Ya Ullah, was that how men lost their minds?

But he wasn't just any man, and he couldn't risk losing his. The repercussions would be unspeakable.

He got to his feet and stormed away, down the steps, tore toward his stables.

If he rode hard enough, fast enough, far enough, he might outrun all the agony and heartache.

Larissa watched Faress receding through solid sheets of tears, her consciousness wavering as anguish pummeled her.

He believed her about the baby being Jawad's. Probably only because he believed she wouldn't be so stupid to lie about something that could be proved so easily. His coldness had barely covered the volcano of precariously leashed resentment and rage, he'd barely treated her with the restraint he thought he owed her as his brother's widow. And if he found out that she wasn't, now that his feelings for her, whatever they were, had been destroyed, worse, reversed, she could lose the baby.

Then just as she'd thought this made it even more vital that he never found out, conceding that anything she suffered was a small price to pay to keep the baby, that she'd try to arrange something with Faress so that the baby would grow up knowing his heritage and, if possible, his family, Faress had delivered the killing blow.

Looking as if he'd turned to stone, as if this was the most repugnant thing he'd ever had to do, he'd made his marriage offer.

At that moment she'd seen into the center of her being.

She'd found it wrapped around the dream she hadn't dared let herself formulate. It had erupted then, fully formed, the dream of belonging to Faress pulverizing her every cell with longing and futility, with imagining every emotion, every sensation, every spark of thought and joy and life of an existence as his wife.

And he'd offered her the dream in the form of a nightmare. It had ruptured her heart.

She was surprised it hadn't for real. But she had the debilitating pain and despondency to thank for stopping her from taking this mess into irretrievable reaches.

They'd stopped her from snatching at his offer, come what may…

"Have you heard the latest catastrophe?" Helal strode into Larissa's office, tossing the rhetorical question around. His answer was the tension in the room rising another notch. Everybody in the kingdom had heard by now. Helal went on, serious, almost agitated, "*B'Ellahi*, first Princess Ghada and now Prince Jawad. I pray this curse doesn't run in threes."

Everybody exchanged uneasy glances. The idea of Faress being the next stricken Aal Rusheed *had* crossed their minds.

Larissa's stomach heaved, her abused heart smashing itself against her ribs as if it would ward off the insupportable dread.

"I heard he was married to an American woman," Tom said. "I don't know why, but I got the impression she didn't survive him."

"If they're both dead," Anika said, shuddering, "thank God they had no children."

"Actually, it's lucky for the non-existent child for another reason," Helal asserted in his all-knowing way. "Other than the kinder fate of being orphaned."

This jogged Larissa from her numbed fugue. She squinted at Helal. "What do you mean?"

Helal elaborated. "If Jawad had fathered a son, by the law of succession of Bidalya, he would have superseded Prince Faress as Crown Prince. And then the king would have fallen on him like he did on Prince Jawad, to mold him into his vision of what a crown prince should be. At least Jawad had a few years of freedom from his father's oppression, and hopefully happiness, before he died. He also had the king for an oppressor when he was a younger and more reasonable man. A child wouldn't have stood a chance."

Larissa regretted asking. She regretted coming to the complex at all today.

She'd come yesterday to check on Jameelah, had kept up a bright façade even knowing it had been goodbye. She should have gone straight to the airport then. But she hadn't been up to making another escape yet. Then she'd found Faress's message on her return to the guest house, demanding her presence at work today.

She'd come running, desperate to see him under any pretext.

Not that she had. She'd found him nowhere.

She'd dragged her feet to her team, and all but Helal had been tactful enough not to ask her about her absence the previous day, and her ravaged appearance now.

They'd just finished their list and she was resigned that Faress had asked her to come only to do the job he was paying her for.

Right now she wasn't up to having her team treat her office as their hangout. She opened her mouth to ask them to leave her alone, closed it. He was here.

Faress. Filling her door, filling her world.

Everything fell away on a wave of searing longing. If only…

"I'll see you in my office," Faress said, his voice clipped, formal, for the first time ignoring the others.

She rose to her feet as if on strings, her team disappearing from her awareness as she followed him.

In minutes she was in his office, all the memories of the best times of her life here, with Faress indulgent and carefree and spontaneous, sweeping through her. Could she one day begin to endure the loss?

He prowled in tight figure eights like a caged lion before her as she slumped on the couch where he always had her sit.

Suddenly he growled, "Why did you refuse my marriage offer?"

The question shot through her heart. The answers almost erupted out of it.

Because you're offering it to a woman who doesn't exist any more, not to me, as a tribute to your brother, a duty to your unborn nephew. Because I can't have you under false pretenses even though I'm dying to have anything of you. Because you only hate me now, would hate me more if you knew the truth…

Instead, her answer was tears gathering in her eyes again.

Faress's black eyes flashed with something like…anxiety? Fear?

Of *course* it was neither. It had to be annoyance with her for resisting his plans when he'd set his mind on them.

Whatever it was, he pressed on, "Larissa, you must reconsider. Think of your baby. You came here looking for his best interests, and this *is* the best thing for him. This is the only way he'll be raised in his privileges and surrounded by his family, with a mother *and* a father."

"A father…?"

"Yes. I will proclaim the baby mine. He will be my heir."

Larissa stared at him, flabbergasted.

She'd automatically assumed he'd be the baby's guardian. She'd thought that he intended later to have heirs with her as she'd already proved fertile, as he'd pointed out, and one fertile woman was as good as another when it came to fulfilling his royal duty.

But he wanted to claim the baby as his first-born heir. Why?

Suddenly Helal's comments flashed in her mind, knocking the breath out of her.

Was it possible he was doing this to stop her baby from preceding him in the succession?

The suspicion lasted all of two seconds. And the verdict was an incontestable *no*. She'd never believe Faress was capable of anything underhanded or petty.

And then even if the baby did have precedence over him, Faress would be acting Crown Prince and, if the king died, regent, until the baby came of age. Not that any of that was even an issue to her.

If Faress proclaimed her baby his, he might not get all of his birthright, but he'd be a prince, would have the family she couldn't give him. And no matter how cold Faress was with her now, any child would be the luckiest on earth to have him as a parent.

But if she told him she wasn't the baby's mother now, he'd rescind his marriage offer. How would he claim the baby then? He could only do that by revealing the truth, that he was Jawad's. And again that would leave the baby motherless. Which was unthinkable.

But he'd already implied that it didn't matter to him who he married as long as she produced heirs, that he only wanted to give the baby both a mother and a father. So would she be committing too huge a crime if she took up his offer to be the baby's mother? Maybe he might even want her again someday…

She raised her abused eyes to his tense, distant face, the face of the stranger he'd become. And she knew. No matter what happened, and even if he wanted her physically, he'd never treat her with tenderness and respect again. If she married him, the only crime she'd be committing would be against herself. She'd be consigning herself to a living hell.

But she didn't matter. Only the baby did.

Feeling like she was jumping into the abyss, she finally nodded.

"You accept?"

His dark, dead voice reverberated in her ears. She nodded again, rasped, "Can you tell me what to expect? What you expect?"

Something agonized seized his noble features. Then it was gone, leaving his face an impassive mask.

His voice was as expressionless when he said, "We will have a ceremony when the forty days of mourning Ghada are over. As for expectations, heirs are what all royal marriages are about. I expect nothing until it's time for a second child."

CHAPTER NINE

"I MUST say it's testament to your progress." Faress inclined his head at the four people milling around him before he transferred his starving eyes to the focus of his world. "And more to your trainer's proficiency that you're here assisting me in one of any surgical team's toughest tests, consecutive surgeries on the same patient."

At his praise, Larissa raised disturbed eyes the blue of his kingdom's twilight skies, lashed him with lust and longing.

She said nothing. She would have before. But she'd stopped talking to him. Beyond necessities and stilted answers to direct questions.

And it had been agony. He'd come to depend on her wit and interaction and counsel for everything from well-being to entertainment to decision-making. Deprived of communication with her, he felt raw, hollowed, cut adrift.

And it was his fault.

Going mad with wanting her, loving her, knowing that she should be taboo to him, with her withdrawal and pain incensing him, more misery crushing him, rejected, guilty, he'd taken refuge in being cold and distant.

She was done appealing to him, had only taken her cue from him. It was as if she turned herself off around him.

Then she'd accepted his proposal as if she had been submitting to a death sentence, had asked what to expect as if asking how he'd carry that sentence out, and his heart, his sanity, had shattered.

Instead of telling her that he'd wait, for ever if need be, until Jawad's memory relinquished its hold over their hearts and psyches, he'd implied that their marriage wouldn't be a real one, ever, that he'd only seek her intimacy to produce heirs.

He'd been trying ever since to retract that insanity. He still couldn't bring himself to voice what he hoped for. Jawad's memory, his own guilt over wanting his woman, his fear of only pushing her to a final, vocal rejection, held him back. So he resorted to actions, showing her that he couldn't get enough of her everywhere in his life. She responded, with something like her former warmth, only around Jameelah…

He tamped down the surge of emotions, for the

thousandth time during the past week questioning the sanity of his decision to continue working together, even more closely than before.

He now included her in all his surgeries, delighting in guiding her to wider fields, astounded at the speed of her uptake, the precision with which she adjusted her surgical knowledge to new procedures, the range of specialties she'd gained experience in before settling on trauma surgery. He even included her team now so she wouldn't spend time away from him. His one excuse was that they were ready, no less than his other secondary assistants.

His gaze caressed her face, regret gnawing him when she averted hers. A rush of oppression flushed through him as he muttered, "A quick review of *Es-Sayedah* Enayat's condition, please, Larissa."

Larissa nodded, snatched her reaction further away from his starving scrutiny, her gaze restless on her team. "*Es-Sayedah* Enayat is a 69-year-old who presented last night with severe chest pain. Investigations revealed blockage of two coronary arteries and carcinoma of the esophago-gastric junction. Faress decided to go for simultaneous transhiatal esophagectomy for tumor removal and an off-pump coronary artery bypass."

"Off-pump?" Helal exclaimed. "Beating-heart surgery? Isn't that still controversial?"

Faress was for once grateful for Helal's contentiousness. It dragged his focus back to his surgical and teaching role, distracted him from counting Larissa's breaths, striving to analyze their cadence for clues to what was going on in the mind she'd closed to him.

Before he could answer Helal, she overtook him, "You think it's safer to employ the conventional cardio-pulmonary bypass? Why? What are the benefits of stopping the heart during surgery?"

Helal cleared his throat, looking like a grade-six student who knew he was about to impress his teacher. "An arrested heart provides surgeons with a still field, no blood while they place the coronary artery grafts, and an empty flaccid heart that can be manipulated easily to expose all coronary branches."

Helal's usual opponent, Anika, spoke up, "Sure, it's easier, surgically speaking, but CPB leads to significant side effects which are cause enough to go for any other viable procedure."

Faress's heart itched in jealousy as Larissa smiled at Anika, one of those smiles of wordless appreciation she'd once lavished on him. It was a good thing she was bestowing it on a woman. A man would have been in grave danger had he been the recipient.

"Exactly," Larissa said. "Those side-effects

resulted in a revival of the beating heart technique. Today up to 20 percent of bypass surgeries are performed off-pump. And with *Es-Sayedah* Enayat, a high-risk patient, it upped off-pump from preferred to indicated."

She snapped a glance at him, asking if she was doing a good job. He wasn't up to anything beyond a nod. He was a half a thought away from grabbing her and ravishing that mouth that so elegantly wrapped around each informed syllable.

Instead, he exhaled, decided to contribute a few insights before they started. "The key to a successful OPCABG is effective cardiac stabilization, reducing cardiac motion either by pressure or suction devices. This is a huge advance from the days when slowing the heart was induced for a quieter heart. Bidalya is making those devices widely available to all GAO surgeons."

"But why are we performing both surgeries at once?" That was Patrick, the bear of a man he now obsessively sought out to discuss Larissa's and the baby's status. "Wouldn't it have been better to remove her cancer first, medically manage her coronary insufficiency, then schedule her for a later bypass?"

Faress looked at Larissa, delegating answering

to her, and was again skewered in the gut by the absence of her vivaciousness, her spontaneity. He wished, each second, that he could erase the past two weeks, return to ignorance, let Jawad live again in his mind and heart, disentangle the memory of his worshipped brother from the reality of his beloved, have his Larissa back.

She inhaled. "From the latest evidence, simultaneous surgeries on a stable patient reduce post-operative and long-term complications. Not to mention cost. As field surgeons they should be your choice whenever possible, to make the most difference to each patient while you can."

Faress considered that perfect wrap-up the ideal point to end the educational session. "We'll go for a curative resection of the lower third of the esophagus and upper third of the stomach," he said. "Then do the CABG next. Larissa and I will keep up a running commentary and I'm sure you won't be shy about asking questions. Be ready to perform any step along the way."

And for the next seven hours, in the tension of an always-precarious endeavor and the exhilaration of being with Larissa in the depth of their element, Faress forgot everything.

During the procedures, he felt Larissa's eyes on him often. Each time he rushed to meet them, anxious for direct contact, only to have them escape, leave his cold and abandoned. But once, at the very end, they didn't.

And what he saw there, the desolation, the yearning…

Ya Rubb, was that how much she mourned Jawad, missed him?

If she'd loved Jawad half as much as *he* loved her, it was.

At that moment, to spare her that much suffering, he wished he'd been the one who'd died.

In another week, Larissa was sure she wouldn't survive.

Ever since Faress had made his intentions clear, her waking and sleeping existence had turned into a parade of nightmares, projecting a life alone as he sought his intimacies elsewhere. Until he needed another heir and came to her, slaked his lust in her body, if only for the purpose of impregnating her, before discarding her again. And she'd have no choice, living for ever in a hell of jealousy and deprivation, for the baby's sake.

She would have surrendered to the despair, adopted it as her new outlook in life, if not for the torment of confusion Faress kept her in.

He kept her closer than ever at work, too close, the man she'd fallen in love with, the leader and healer to be followed, worshipped, once again extending her public esteem, focusing on her with an intensity that seared her soul with a deeper brand of ownership, even made her hope he might be considering making the best of the compromise he'd made. Yet he said nothing. And she couldn't survive the insecurity, the uncertainty for much longer…

"I can't put it off any longer."

Larissa's heart contracted, wouldn't expand again. *Faress.*

Oh, God. She'd been staring at him all along. But now he'd spoken, she didn't have to ask him to elaborate.

Jameelah was ready to be discharged. It was time to tell her.

She gulped down an upsurge of scorching pity, nodded.

"Will you be with me?"

Oh, God, the way he'd said that! The sheer depth of need, dread and suffering!

And if that was all he needed from her, solace and support, it would be enough. It was a good enough cause.

She could stop herself from reaching out to him as easily as she could stop her heart. She took his hand, squeezed it between both of hers. His jaw muscles bunched. Then his other hand enveloped both of hers in the grip of a man clinging to a lifeline, the pressure assuaging, engulfing, emptying her heart of blood, filling her with strength for him to draw on, to supplement his boundless one.

A long, full glance told her he understood, and appreciated it.

Then he turned and walked with her to Jameelah's suite.

Larissa was no stranger to horrific emotional injury and loss. With all her loved ones dead, with the only man she'd ever love alienated for ever, she thought nothing could be more brutal.

Then came the harrowing chore of informing Jameelah that she'd lost her remaining parent.

All else seemed to pale in comparison.

She felt Faress's echoing devastation as they struggled to contain Jameelah's first explosion of denial and grief, the hysterical accusations that they were lying, the screams for her mother, the manic struggles to run in search of her. They restrained her, sedated her, huddled over her, warding off what they could of her agony.

After the first tidal wave had wrung the weeping

girl dry, she and Faress sat next to her on the bed, forming an impenetrable shield around her, caressing and soothing her. Then as the girl sagged into their embrace, surrendered to shock and exhaustion and chemical relief, Larissa raised her eyes to Faress's. And the tears that had just slowed down gushed again.

His face was wet, his eyes reflecting the hell his niece had been plunged into. With a cry of distress she reached a quaking hand to his face, wiping away his tears. He surrendered to her ministrations, pressed his face into her palm, a deep groan bleeding from his chest. Their eyes meshed in deepest empathy, in communion.

Then he reached for her, his large hand cupping her head, bunching in her hair, transfixing her. Then he took her, fused her to him, his tongue seeking her passion and life, devouring her, invading her, demanding that she join her flesh to his, that she surrender all her pain and take his, share it, halve it, exorcize it.

Then, just as it started, it ended.

He withdrew, breathing hard, his eyes scorching down at her, passion and pain staining his every feature. Then his eyes clouded on another brand of pain, one that left her gasping with confusion and anxiety, before withdrawal stole any flicker of emotion from them. He tore them away and she plummeted in a void of deprivation as he curved his body around Jameelah.

Choking on her pulped heart, she withdrew her arms from the sleeping girl, relinquished her to his care.

At the edge of the bed, Faress's hand clamped her arm, gentle, fierce, inexorable, tugged her back.

Nerveless, she fell back on the bed as he sat up, dwarfing both her and Jameelah. In heartbreaking tenderness he curved her and Jameelah together until they were almost a single entity. Then he came around, stretched his formidable body behind her, slipped his arms and legs beneath and above them, containing them both in his all-encompassing embrace.

She lay inundated by him, hugged around Jameelah, her tears a constant stream wetting the girl's hair, trickling down her now sunken cheek, trembling for hours as Faress stroked bonding pathways between their huddled bodies, his protection flowing in caresses over her and both ravaged and unborn child of his lost siblings, alternating ragged kisses between her and Jameelah, murmuring Arabic of such complexity she understood none of it beyond the certainty that it was prayers. And pledges.

* * *

"You must promise first!"

Larissa gazed up at the beautiful sight before her, her heart booming in thankfulness. Two weeks after her discharge from hospital, Jameelah, resilient and intensively nurtured by her and Faress, was back to normal. Physically at least.

In a palest yellow cotton silk *jalabeyah*, her mahogany hair hanging in glossy waves down to her hips and surrounding a face of smoothest olive skin and loveliest features, she was now standing over her, somber, demanding her promise for her honest opinion of some of her artwork. Before she ventured to show her any.

"I promise, *ya habibati*," Larissa said, the endearment as usual flowing from her heart. "I will always tell you the truth."

The girl gave her the uncertain look of someone who was loath to expose her dabbling to others yet longing for feedback and deciding to throw caution to the wind.

Larissa watched her spin around, gathering her long *jalabeyah* in one hand as she rushed to her activity room, her every move and line a pleasure to watch, her every breath a reason for gratitude.

Ever since she'd had the privilege of helping to save her life, she'd forged a profound connection to her, formed of Jameelah's bond with Faress,

Jameelah's own exquisite nature and the pull of her own blood now coursing in Jameelah's system. And she knew the connection was reciprocated.

She'd come to know so much about her in the past two weeks, every day bringing more proof of sensitivity, brilliance and thoughtfulness that were rare, not only at her age but in anyone of any age. Larissa also got glimpses of her wit, sensed her innate exuberance. But those were now buried. It would take much longer for those traits to resurface.

She'd been with her at Faress's palace every day, adjusting her schedule for breakfasts together every morning and early enough dinners to allow for a couple of hours before Jameelah's bedtime every night. In part, she'd been reveling in her company, in another, striving to tide her over the worst of her mourning.

And Jameelah had tided her over the worst of hers.

That had been until Faress had also adjusted his schedule and became a constant part of their time together.

She craved having him near, but she'd almost demanded he leave her alone with Jameelah, to make his own time with her. It was too much, having him in such proximity, in such an emotional, family-like setting. For there, for Jameelah's sake, he reverted to the spontaneous, indulgent man he'd been, including her in his cosseting of Jameelah.

Then when Jameelah left for bed, he reached for her, as if compelled, his touch tinged with an obsession that ignited hers, his kisses draining her of reason and essence, only to pull away, a look of regret and revulsion twisting his face.

She stumbled deeper in chaos, obsessing over explanations.

She only came up with one. Each time his unappeased hunger for her body overcame his discretion and intentions, he ended up hating her more, hating himself for his lapses. But he'd later remember that she was too valuable to him, if only for his dead siblings' children, and he'd resume his efforts to return to warmth and ease with her. Until the next kiss…

But what made her suffering and turmoil fade into insignificance was Jameelah. And the baby growing inside her. They were the suns in the perpetual night her existence had turned into.

"Hadi walla hadi?"

Larissa stirred with a jerk, instantly translating Jameelah's question in her mind. This or this?

She marveled at both paintings. And bled at both. They showed such talent, such a sense of balance and beauty, such an eye for detail and a hand capable of translating what that eye perceived. But the pain there, the loss…

One was of an empty bedroom, a woman's, full of everything that spoke of taste and prosperity, everything arranged in painful order, indicating no life there, turning the bedroom into a shrine. The other was of a cliff overlooking the sea with a little girl sitting there alone, tiny and lost in the vastness.

Fighting the suffocation of pity, she forced tears back and pleasure in Jameelah's artwork to surface on her face. "*Habibati*, they are each a masterpiece."

Jameelah's black eyes faltered on uncertainty, then a sparkle lit their depths. "Really?"

"They would be for someone twice your age. But they're unbelievable for a ten-year-old. When did you complete them?"

"At school. I can't go to physical education classes since… since the accident, so I go to the art room."

"You should go more often. Do you have more work?"

"Loads." Suddenly she wilted, tears blossoming in her eyes. "Mama had loads of paintings too, but hers are like magic. She's the one who taught me how to draw and paint. She was teaching me how to do perspective and shadows before…before…"

Larissa hugged her, kissed her eyes, wiped away the tears that had escaped, the tears that always seemed poised to brim over. "And she taught you so well, and now every time you put a pencil or a brush to paper or canvas, you'll make magic, too. And every time people look at it, they'll feel happy, like I am now. Your mother gave you an incredible gift."

Jameelah stared at her with those eyes that so resembled Faress's, as if trying to decide if she could believe all that.

Then a tremulous smile broke on her dimpled lips. "So you don't have a preference?"

"Actually, I do. But it's not because it's better drawn. They're both amazing. But the cliff scene is so incredible, you make me feel the salt wind on the girl's face and in her hair, the rumble of the waves breaking on the rocks, the heat of the sun beating down on her. It's as if it's all real."

"It is real. It's…it *was* Mama's favorite place in all the kingdom."

"You see?" Larissa rushed on to interrupt Jameelah's renewed agitation. "You re-created it so faithfully you did more than make it *look* real.

A photo does that. You made it *feel* real. You are a true artist."

Jameelah's wobbling chin stilled as Larissa talked. Then it started again. "It's called Ras Algam. Mama went there with Baba, then when he died and I grew up, she took me…"

And there was no question the girl sitting huddled under the outcrop of rock was Jameelah, left behind in the world by both her parents. Larissa hugged her again, trying to control the gush of emotion. "Will you take me some time?"

Jameelah blinked, the tears receding. "You want to go?"

"I'd love to go. Can we have a picnic?"

Jameelah's brightness dimmed again. "By the time I'm well enough and autumn comes, when we can go, you may be gone."

Larissa wanted to cry that she'd never go, that she'd always be there for her. But the promises caught in her throat.

She had no way of knowing if she would be. Thirty-six days of Ghadah's forty days' mourning period had passed and Faress hadn't mentioned any preparations. He hadn't even mentioned his offer again.

He'd probably decided to withdraw it, was

thinking of some other way to keep his brother's son. He'd probably realized he couldn't tie himself to a woman he didn't love. He must be thinking of when he finally met the woman he wanted to marry and have children with, what an injury he would have done her and himself tying himself, for whatever reason, to Larissa.

Even if he went through with his plans, she might not be able to survive being near him and estranged from him. She might end up running away. How could she promise the bereaved girl that she'd stay, when she might end up leaving her, too?

"*Khali* Faress!"

Larissa jerked at Jameelah's exclamation. She'd been staring at her as she'd struggled for something truthful to say, now saw her dejection dissolve in the sheer pleasure that was reserved for Faress.

She swung around, her heart shaking her apart as Jameelah rushed to meet him, swallowed the surge of longing as he opened his arms wide, his stride eating up the ground to contain Jameelah that much sooner. But what slashed her was his smile, so welcoming and unfettered. A smile he'd once lavished on her. Never again.

"Kaif Jameelati?"

Her heart fired. Her eyes flew in a shock of hope to his, met them over Jameelah's head and realized. He'd meant Jameelah. He was asking how his beautiful one was.

He kept his eyes on her as he hugged Jameelah with as much exuberance as she hugged him. Then with utmost care for her recent injuries, he swung her up in his arm, walked toward Larissa with Jameelah clinging around his neck, her head buried in his chest. It was clear Faress had always been her most loved relative after her mother, the man who'd been her father figure all along.

He sat down beside Larissa, and every cell in her body surged at his nearness as he took Jameelah nestling into him, threw his other arm along the couch's back, an inch from Larissa's. In a moment his arm obliterated that inch.

It lay there on her shoulder, as if waiting for something. The shudder that shook her seemed to be it. His arm tightened, drawing her into him, hugging her as he did Jameelah, sat sweeping caresses over them.

She lay in his embrace, enervated, listening to the most potent, world-shaking sound she'd ever heard. His heartbeats.

He sighed, a sound of contentment playing havoc with hers, tilted both her and Jameelah's faces up to him. "So what have my ladies been up to in the two hours they managed to have without me?"

She stopped herself from surging to catch his words in her lips somehow. Next second, mortification clogged her throat.

She *would* end up begging him. And when he rejected her…

Jameelah hugged him more securely. "We've been starving."

He exhaled. "Don't make me feel more guilty than I already am, *ya sagheerati*. Keeping you waiting was something many people found out I don't take kindly to tonight."

Larissa's heart itched at the remorse in his voice. She'd already known any child, anyone, would be the luckiest person on earth to have Faress's love. But the full scope of that luck was unfolding with each moment, each word, each action. And she couldn't bear it that he might be thinking he'd let Jameelah down even fleetingly. She had to rid him of any shadow of discomfort.

She breathed, "Actually, we couldn't decide what to eat."

He chuckled, his heavy-lidded gaze now focused on lips still tingling with the kiss she hadn't dared to take.

"Never fear. I'm here to feed my girls." He turned to Jameelah. "How about we raid the kitchen and whip up something Larissa has never eaten before?"

Jameelah sat up, her eyes brightening. "Can we make *harees*? And *maasoob* for dessert?"

Faress laughed. "*Maasoob* is in, *harees* is out, if we want to eat tonight." He turned to Larissa, explained, "*Maasoob* is *khobez*, cut in small pieces, mashed with banana and sugar and caramelized in butter. Done in minutes. *Harees* is veal and chicken cooked with whole wheat and a dozen spices and then served on fried crunchy *khobez*. Very tasty, but it takes hours, maybe a whole day."

"Now I'm really starving!" Larissa exclaimed.

"We can make *matazeez* instead," Jameelah suggested. "It has meat and tomato sauce and okra and aubergine and courgette and this stuff that looks like ravioli…"

"Oh, please, stop," Larissa moaned. "I'll eat anything now."

Laughing again, Faress heaved up to his feet, pulling them both up. "Let's take pity on Larissa, Jameelah, and not tell her about *el marassee*, *el aggut*, and *el gareesh*."

Jameelah was excited now, as alive as Larissa had ever seen her. "We can make them on Friday when we have all day!"

At the mention of Friday, she met his eyes, saw his instant awareness of what it was. Their supposed wedding day.

Seeing tension leaping back in his eyes again, she knew.

He'd decided not to go ahead with it. But he still hadn't found an acceptable alternative. He wanted Jawad's baby, and he wanted her to be Jameelah's surrogate parent with him. And he wanted her body. And he still couldn't come up with a solution that didn't include marriage to assure him of having all that.

On realizing she'd sunk so far she'd been yearning to become his sham wife, now wanted to offer to be anything else so she'd be with him and the children, the world that had brightened with the magic of his ease and seeming return to intimacy dimmed again.

CHAPTER TEN

"THE packs are stuck. More saline please, Anika," Faress murmured.

Anika at once complied, soaking the packs around the liver so Faress could remove them without yanking on the fragile tissues, causing renewed hemorrhage.

"Turn up the heat, Tom, please," Larissa said without removing her eyes from his fingers. Tom pushed up the dial of the electric blanket their patient lay on. "And raise IV fluid temperature to 108 degrees."

"Two more units packed red blood cells and coagulation factors," Helal told one of the nurses. He was one of the team now working on a patient with multiple abdominal injuries.

Faress nodded his corroboration and the nurse hastened to comply. Hypothermia and coagulation failure and the vicious circle of deterioration they initiated were the cause of death in multiple abdominal trauma. No care to avoid their development was too much. Larissa and her team were going by the book.

"I still can't believe *Es-sayed* Anan here lasted through the first stage of damage control surgery," Patrick said as he helped Faress remove the last of the packs. "And is now well enough to be back for definitive repairs just a day later."

Larissa's team had had their first unassisted, unsupervised surgery yesterday when Larissa hadn't been able to come to work. Another pile-up on the highway had made Faress decide to test them out with three surgeries he thought Larissa had well prepared them for. They'd come through with flying colors.

"Perfect first-stage management, Tom, Helal, Patrick, Anika," Faress said after he and Larissa finished exploring the abdomen. "We wouldn't have done better."

"Thanks", "Yeah, we're good", "We were *lucky*" and "We just have the best trainer" were murmured in succession, a true reflection of each respondent's character.

Then silence fell as they collaborated on working on one of the man's injuries. Faress worked with Patrick and Tom on the intestinal injuries, Larissa, Helal and Anika took the spleen.

When they came to the hardest and most delicate part of the surgery, the removal of the vascular shunt, the rest left him and Larissa to it, went back to lesser assisting roles.

"Medial rotation of the liver, Anika," Faress murmured.

"Suction. And more exposure of the portal triad, Tom." Larissa's request was tranquil, her movements as she repaired the vessels a blur of fluency and assurance.

He could hardly believe that just yesterday he'd exploded to Larissa's side with nightmares crashing in his head, transporting a lab's and investigative unit's worth of portable kits and instruments to her bedside, not even thinking of taking Patrick with him. His heart still stopped when he remembered how he'd found her lying there pale and too scared to move.

It had taken both of the experienced surgeons a frantic time and every investigation they could think of to realize she hadn't been miscarrying but had had a touch of enteritis, which had responded promptly to mild medications.

The relief, the poignancy of knowing Jawad's baby was safe, that she was, had given way to the arousal of being near her on the bed he'd once lain in absorbing her echoes, with her now in it shaken, relieved, equally aroused…

Only the memory of her depressed apprehension when Friday—which was now tomorrow—had come up that night with Jameelah had stopped him from reaching for her.

He'd been waiting for her to express the least interest in his plans for their upcoming marriage ceremony. But she evidently still thought of the event with the same resignation of serving a life sentence.

"Warm, stable. He's going to be fine. He's all yours, guys. Close him up."

Larissa's assessment dragged his focus back to the moment, made him step back to join her in watching the others perform a meticulous closure. Afterwards they checked their patient's vital signs then Anika and another nurse took him to IC and Larissa walked ahead with the rest of her team to the soiled room.

He followed, devouring her as she stripped off her scrubs, her clothes stretching over her curves, clinging to her, the barely detectable mound where her baby was growing healthy and strong, her bun unraveling, her hair thudding down her back…

It was no good. He *was* going out of his mind. This was far stronger than he was. And each night he succumbed, snatched her in his arms, against his resolutions and good intentions. And each time she responded and he'd forget anything had ever gone wrong between them. Then he'd see that haunted, pained look in her eyes, and he'd have a reality check.

Feeling guilty and heartsick, he forced himself to withdraw. And burned. He shouldn't be craving her every minute of every day like that. He despised his weakness, couldn't help but have episodes of bitterness towards her for engendering it in him, for wanting him so soon, for only wanting him and not loving him.

Then he shared with her again and she conquered him again. Then she went further, extended her healing and generosity to his bereaved Jameelah, and gave her, and him, in the times of closeness and poignancy they spent together, a family, a renewed will to live. Now he had a taste of what was to come, he wanted it all, the family, the children, her, body and soul…

The forty days were over today. He'd intended to inform his father of his plans long before now. But he hadn't yet made them. He couldn't bring himself to with Larissa in this state. Couldn't bring himself to tell her that if she didn't want their marriage to be real eventually, she had to say no. Couldn't risk she'd say it.

But he wouldn't marry her and remain away from her. Jawad's memory wouldn't hold him back for ever, but if it would her, she'd better...

"Dr. Faress, Dr. Larissa..." A nurse came in, panting. "*Ameerah* Jameelah is in the prep room."

He tore his eyes from the nurse, sought Larissa's, shared his shock. Then they exploded in motion.

In a minute they entered the hall where surgical cases were prepped before being rushed to the OR, found Jameelah standing in the middle of the floor, looking smaller, lost.

Larissa's breath was knocked out of her at the sight of Jameelah.

She'd been crying, her eyes swollen, feverish.

Oh God, what was wrong now?

She reached her first, swept her in a fierce hug. "*Habibati*, are you OK?"

Jameelah nodded as Faress took them to one side of the hall.

"How did you get here, *ya sagheerati*?" he asked, his voice gentleness and indulgence itself.

"I told Hassan to drive me here after school." She looked up at Larissa with wavering eyes. "I—I wanted to make sure you remembered our—our cooking date tomorrow..."

Larissa's heart convulsed. "Of course, I do."

"It's just you didn't come yesterday..."

"I was sick, *ya habibati*." She'd woken up with cramps, and they'd sent her crying for Faress. Not Patrick. When she'd needed help, he was all she'd been able to think of. She still couldn't believe the speed with which he'd responded, the mini-hospital he'd transferred to her bedside, the magnitude of his anxiety.

It had turned out to be nothing, but he'd insisted she stay in bed the rest of the day. They couldn't be too careful. She'd agreed. She'd been useless anyway in the aftermath of anxiety, and the further blow of having him so caring only to have him withdraw again.

"But you didn't come for breakfast today," Jameelah insisted.

That sounded like an accusation. She had to tread carefully. "I was tired after yesterday. I woke up after you went to school."

Jameelah was ready with an argument. "But you came to work."

Larissa measured her words. They were the truth, but she had to be careful how to phrase it. "I woke up feeling better and, knowing you were at school, I came here. And I'll come home right after work. And tomorrow we have a date, a whole day together, like every weekend, *ya habibati*. I can't wait for your *gareesh*."

"You may be sick again," Jameelah mumbled.

"I won't be. It was nothing serious. But, darling, please…"

At that moment the doors whooshed open and an incoming casualty was wheeled in. At the sight of the woman on the gurney, Larissa's blood froze. Her external injuries were extensive. And she had an uncanny general resemblance to Ghadah.

A glance at Faress showed his equal dread what this might do to Jameelah's fragile mental condition. She tore her eyes away, rushed Jameelah out of the room, feeling Faress rushing after them, being detained at the door.

"Was Mama hurt like that?" Jameelah's voice wobbled, her tears streaming again.

"No, no," Larissa groaned. "It was inside she was hurt. But she didn't suffer."

"Will *Khali* Faress operate on the hurt woman?"

"Yes, *ya habibati*, but you must go home now…"

Jameelah clung to her just as Faress exploded out into the corridor to join them. "Come with me."

Just as Faress's hand squeezed her shoulder, telling her he didn't need her there now, Anika came out of the hall, running.

"Dr. Faress, Dr. Larissa—she has cardiac tamponade, already fibrillated once!"

Larissa knew the emergency thoracotomy needed

for that was one procedure her team wasn't proficient in yet, and no other surgeon was free to give Faress the help he'd need. She exchanged desperate looks with Faress. He gave her a terse nod.

"Prep her. We're coming," Larissa called back, then turned to Jameelah. "*Habibati*, I have to take care of that woman."

"So when will you be home?"

"I don't know exactly when we'll finish…"

Insecurity and panic flared in Jameelah's eyes. "You're not coming, are you? You're not coming to see me ever again!"

Faress tried to intervene. "Jameelah, that is not true. We're both coming home right after we finish here."

Jameelah turned eyes full of fear and accusation on him. "You're just saying that. You didn't come yesterday either."

"I was with Larissa, treating her—"

Jameelah's cry cut him off. *"You'll stop coming, too."*

Larissa's heart gave a sickening lurch as she met Faress's anguished gaze. He went down on his haunches, bringing his eyes level with Jameelah's. "I'm never going to stop coming, *ya sagheerati*. But this woman will die if we don't help her. And you want us to help her, don't you?"

Jameelah looked from him to Larissa then burst out crying.

Faress hugged her. “We’ll send you home now, *ya Jameelati*, and we’ll come rushing to you as soon as we’re done.”

Larissa surrounded her with Faress, bent to kiss her, whispered the promise, “Both of us.”

Feeling Jameelah’s tension drain away, Faress straightened, barked orders arranging for both her return home and the surgery. Larissa stood long enough to see Jameelah being escorted out then raced with Faress to tend their casualty in a blur of urgency.

It was three hours before they rushed back to the palace, their trip an even more agitated experience than their daily ones had become.

Minutes before they arrived, Faress received a phone call that turned him to stone beside her.

He barked something explosive then snapped his phone shut.

He turned to her, his eyes wild. “Jameelah has disappeared.”

They arrived to chaos. All the invisible people Larissa sensed and never saw were swarming over the palace grounds.

A man in black, clearly Faress's security co-ordinator, came rushing up to them.

"You will all answer for letting her slip your surveillance," Faress hissed, dread making him frightening. Larissa shuddered, her already compromised composure teetering. Faress gathered her to him, bolstering her.

The fierce-looking man bent his head, unable to meet Faress's volcanic gaze. "*Somo'ak*... Her guards just returned. They lost track of her car on the way from the complex, thought Hassan had sped ahead. When they arrived here to find she hadn't arrived, they combed the city, hoping to find her. They didn't, had to come clean. As Hassan didn't try to alert them, we're suspecting a plot, a kidnapping."

"Then you're fools as well as incompetents," Faress growled. "Insight into people's characters is a security professional's number-one asset and since you're clearly lacking in it, it's time we re-evaluated your careers, Bassel. Hassan worshipped *Ameerah* Ghadah, dotes on Jameelah. He'd give his life for them. Why do you think I trusted him with them in the first place? Don't compound your negligence. Find her."

Then with Larissa flying in his wake, he exploded into a desperate search for her himself, contacting his extensive family, ordering each member to search for her, turning her quarters inside out for clues, his anger and suspicion rising by the second as he expanded the search from a local to a national one.

At one point he groaned to Larissa, "If only it was an abduction, I'd be sure to get her back. Enemies would know not to harm her, and that I'd pay of my flesh to get her back."

But no calls came. There was silence, ignorance. Nothing.

After a horrific night of futility, dawn came.

Faress was standing by Jameelah's bedroom window, rigid, staring out at skies turning indigo.

Larissa watched him, her tears internal now, drenching her soul. She wouldn't show him her tears. And she wouldn't cry for Jameelah. She was fine. She *had* to be.

But she couldn't bear feeling his guilt, his dread destroying him all over again. She would have multiplied hers a hundred times if she could only have spared him.

"That night I came late," he suddenly said, his voice a bass grate of anguish. "I stood in the doorway and watched you. You were so absorbed in what you were discussing, you weren't aware of me. I couldn't hear you either, not what you were saying, just your murmuring and cooing. And it was the most beautiful thing I've ever seen, ever heard. That night I thought, Ghadah can find peace, knowing the daughter she lived for won't be lost with her death. Now I may have really lost her…"

Larissa raced to him, her arms convulsing around him from the back, cried, "You won't lose her, we won't." She staggered back. He swung around, reached for her, anxiety blazing on his face. She reached back, gripped both his arms. "I think I know where she is. That night she showed me a painting she made of her mother's favorite place. It's called…called… Oh, God…"

His eyes feverish with hope, he ran calming hands over her head and face. "Breathe, *ya habibati*, concentrate."

She racked her brains. Then it came to her in a flash. "It's Ras Al… Ras Al…"

His obsidian eyes flashed. "Ras Algam?"

She jumped in his arms. "*Yes*. That is *it*. I have a feeling she went there, to feel close to her mother."

Hope solidified into certainty in his eyes as he grabbed her arm, already running. "Let's find her."

They found her. They also found out how she'd made it there. Her driver, Hassan had driven her there.

At seeing Faress, he fell to his knees before him.

"Ameerah Ghadah came to me in my sleep," Hassan sobbed. "She told me she wanted to see her daughter. And when Jameelah asked to come here, on the fortieth night of her mother's passing, I knew this is where and when *Ameerah* Ghadah wanted to see her. The night was still and warm and I thought *ameerati es-sagheerah* would be safe here. I had blankets and food in the car and I promised not to tell you before noon. I know my punishment will be severe…"

"Silence," Faress ground out, his face shuttered on extreme control, his eyes feverish on the cliff where Jameelah was a barely visible sleeping heap. "I'll see to you later."

Then he was striding to the cliff.

Larissa kept up with him. "She came last night looking for me, Faress. I was the one to whom she showed the painting of this place, the one she fears will abandon her. Her crisis right now is focusing on her mother and me. And, knowing her, this isn't a cry for attention. This is serious. Let me go to her, alone."

Faress looked down at Larissa. In the sunlight reflected off the stormy sea and white sand, though pale and exhausted, she took his breath, his soul away.

And he conceded her point. With Jameelah this vulnerable, it was the woman who'd started to fill the void of Ghadah's loss who was the most likely to get favorable results.

He took her hand, pressed a kiss laden with gratitude into her palm, nodded. She gave him a wobbly smile then turned and strode up the slope leading to the cliff.

In minutes she was up there. His heart thundered as he watched Jameelah waking up, scrambling to her feet and rushing away from Larissa's solicitude. And close to the edge. Too close.

And he ran, breathless, keeping out of sight, scared out of his mind that his appearance and any more agitation might tip Jameelah over the edge.

He circled them, climbed on top of the outcrop of rock overlooking the recess where Jameelah had spent the night. He was calculating he could take the fifteen-foot jump, reach Jameelah in under five seconds, if the worst came to the worst, when he heard Larissa's voice. Compassion incarnate.

"Your mother loved you, even when she was late or away. It's the same with me and Faress. We'll always come back to you."

"No, you won't. *Mama is never coming back*

now," Jameelah cried, her usually tranquil voice shrill.

Larissa kept her voice soothing. "No one can beat death, *ya habibati*. But it will take that to take us away from you."

"So you won't mean to leave me, but you will, like Baba and Mama. And if death will take everyone away and then me, why shouldn't it take me now?"

Faress's heart burst with the need to jump down and snatch her away from the edge. That wasn't a hypothetical question. She *was* contemplating it. Larissa had been right about the necessity of treating her with the caution of defusing a bomb.

But how would she defuse such an explosive question?

"We all know we'll die, *ya habibati,* and it makes life so much more precious," Larissa said seriously, no trace of condescension in her words or voice. "And we want to live it with the people we love. And it is horrible and heartbreaking that you lost your parents. But life gives as well as takes. You're much better off than most people still. You can do so many things in your life, make such a difference to the world, help so many people, like your mother did. You're a princess, you have a family…"

Jameelah stomped her feet over and over in a fit of frustration. "I *don't*. They pretended to care about me to please Mama, and now to please *Khali* Faress. Everyone else is paid to be nice to me, or they want something from being nice to me. I only have *Khali* and now you…maybe…"

Faress's heart compressed. She'd realized the burden of being royalty too early. *Ya Ullah*, what would Larissa say to that?

"You have me, no maybes," she said, her voice brooking no argument. "And it *is* enough to have only one or two people in the world who truly love you, *ya habibati*. And you never lose the people you love when they die. They're still with you, part of who you are. I lost my mother and father at the same time and I still remember and love everything about them. I was older than you are now but I had no one to truly love but my sister. Then I lost her, too, just before I came to Bidalya. But God is giving me what's making her loss bearable. A baby."

"A baby? You mean you're having a baby?" Jameelah looked her up and down in stupefaction. "But your belly isn't big!"

"Oh, it will get bigger and bigger now." Larissa's hands stroked her stomach lovingly. Faress's whole being seized with love and tenderness, for her and for the baby growing inside her. She took a step towards Jameelah, who took an instinctive step back. That froze Larissa, almost burst Faress's head in fright. The only thing that stopped him from jumping was knowing that five seconds wouldn't be enough if Jameelah took one more step back.

Larissa looked around, as if she was struggling for the best thing to say now. Then she exhaled. "I want to share a secret with you, Jameelah. Can you promise to keep it?" Jameelah nodded warily. "My baby is a boy, and he's your cousin."

After a moment of incomprehension, the most amazing transformation came over Jameelah's face. "He's *Khali* Faress's!"

Larissa hesitated just a second before nodding. "Now you'll have another person to love and who'll love you. You'll be his big sister and I'll need all your help with him. And there's one thing you can give him that I can't. I'm hopeless at art and I so hope you'll teach him the magic that your mother taught you."

Faress squeezed his eyes, an agony of love and pride and gratitude for all that Larissa was and did clamping his chest, would have brought him to his knees if he wasn't already on them. She'd found the only thing to drag Jameelah from the abyss of despair. A focus outside herself, someone to nurture, a cause.

Sure enough, Jameelah's tears dried, her face coming alive as she bombarded Larissa with questions. "When will you have him? Can I suggest names for him? Please, don't call him Omar or Fahad. I have *six* atrocious second cousins with those names."

Still asking questions, Jameelah moved away from the edge. Larissa rushed to meet her halfway. Faress began to breathe again.

And it all happened at once.

The cliff edge crumbled beneath Jameelah's feet. She screamed, stumbled, fell flat on her face. A shout rang out of Larissa as she lunged after her, caught both her wrists at the last moment. Faress exploded into motion, felt his muscles tearing, saw nothing but Larissa beginning to slide with Jameelah's weight and the rolling rocks beneath her, didn't even feel the impact this time when he flung himself after her, clamped her ankles.

He pulled them back, their combined weight nothing to the force of his love, snatching them, the two who made up his world, from danger.

He carried them to safety, his arms convulsing around them, his lips spilling a fever of gratitude and love all over them.

They both buried themselves in his chest and wept.

* * *

"She's still sleeping." Faress turned to Larissa as he closed Jameelah's door. She'd fallen asleep on the way back and hadn't stirred when he'd carried her to bed.

Larissa nodded, lingering shock in her eyes, wringing his heart. He bent and swept her up in his arms.

She clung to him all the way to his quarters, her head on his heart, alive and unharmed. *Ya Ullah*, alive, unharmed.

He could have lost her. She would have given her life to save Jameelah. And he would have only flung himself after her and all that remained of his siblings.

And he knew. There wasn't the tiniest bit of jealousy or bitterness left in him that fate had chosen to make her Jawad's before him. His love had grown truly unconditional.

And there was no guilt either. His brother had loved her beyond reason, for every reason, as she deserved to be loved. And so did he. Jawad had lived for her, had died in her arms, and, knowing him, the all-loving man he'd been, he would have wanted her to live her life to the full, to find love and passion again. And she had, with him, and it no longer mattered how fast it had happened. It had, and he wasn't postponing making her his, becoming hers, one more minute. Seconds had ended

Ghadah's life, could have lost him Larissa and everything he lived for. Each minute was no longer something he could afford to waste, waiting on the caprices of custom or the insubstantial rites of guilt.

The time was now. And for ever.

He placed her in reverence on his bed, his eyes never leaving hers in the lights he kept dimmed to counteract the glare of the rest of his existence, saw them reflecting the turbulence of the sea where he'd almost lost her today.

With a moan warding off the memory, he came down half over her, needing to feel her, her life, her reality. Memories crashed inside him still, of every moment he'd known her, of the only time he'd had her here, the heart-bursting expectation of pleasure beyond his knowledge and her overwhelming surrender.

This time she didn't surrender, she went far beyond overwhelming him. She sabotaged his reason, surging into him, bringing him fully over her, taking the brunt of his passion, containing it in limbs that clamped him body and will, fingers that unraveled his flesh and control, meeting his crushing kiss halfway, her lips, full and fragrant, mashing against his, her tongue invading his mouth in turn, flooding him with her taste and her passion, snatching at his, turning the kiss into a full rehearsal of the mating they'd soon lose themselves in, multiplying its force, deepening its madness, sharpening its pleasure to pain.

He thrust at her, tongue and loins, blind, out of his mind, heard his frenzy harmonizing with hers in a duet of rising voracity. She thrust back, offering, demanding, undulating beneath him, her heat even through their clothes igniting consecutive fuses inside him, until their mimicking of their love act turned into distress, writhing desperation. He was overloading, she was…

He tore his lips from hers, roared at the separation, at the convulsion that went through her with his loss, at the sight of the full measure of his ferocity, his insanity reflected in the depths of eyes gone purple. He shuddered in unison with her with arousal turned into agony, the need for fusion becoming damage.

One shaking hand gathered both of hers when they reached for him, dug into his flesh, tugged at his hair, hurrying his impact, imprisoning them above her head. His other tore her out of her clothes, shredded what slowed him down, the rising music of her cries of stimulation, of impatience urging him on.

Then she was naked beneath him, velvet resilience and total hunger sending the beast inside him howling. He swooped down on her, mouth clamping nipples larger than before, darker, better instruments for her torment and pleasure, for his, hands kneading riper breasts. Her cries became keens fractured by indrawn distress, her hands lurching out of his containment, grabbing at him, shattering the last of his restraint. He boosted her pressure, mashed his face into her mounds, into the firmness of her abdomen that had barely begun to succumb to the expansion of pregnancy…

An image hit him like a gut punch with its clarity, its tangibility. Larissa, riper, bigger, with him kneeling between her thighs, thrusting, caressing her womb from inside with his manhood as he caressed it from outside with his hands…

Growling incoherently, he rose over her, tore his shirt off flesh that would burn if it didn't mesh with hers, now…*now*. One hand went to release himself, the other dipping two fingers inside her, all he could do in his extreme to ascertain her readiness.

She flinched as if he'd stabbed her, grabbed his hand.

Then her sob tore through him. "Faress…I *can't…*"

He blinked, paralyzed with the sight of pain and panic flooding her face. Blood crashed against the walls of his arteries with the sudden halt, making the world flicker, his hands shake as he forced both to withdraw, one from his body, one from hers.

But he couldn't accept her rejection this time. Her desire for him was indisputable, and her emotions were involved. With her reticence with him from day one, he had no idea how involved they were, could only hope for a fraction of his own involvement.

All that was left was for him to dispel her demons as he'd dispelled his, release her from the shackles of guilt and make her embrace their new life together.

"Larissa," he started, his breathing labored, frustration shredding through him, the need to see her delirious and open for him once more an even bigger pain. "I know, as Jawad's widow…"

She twisted in his arms as if he'd backhanded her, looked up at him as if she expected an axe would swing down and lodge in her heart.

Then she rasped, "I'm not."

CHAPTER ELEVEN

"I'M NOT his widow," she repeated, her whisper thicker, more impeded. Faress stared at her, certain his mind had disintegrated. Her trembling hand reached for the cover, dragged it over her nakedness. "The photograph you saw, that was my sister, Claire. She looked almost like my twin. She was Jawad's wife."

He staggered up to his feet.

Larissa wasn't Jawad's. *She wasn't Jawad's.*

Before the elation had a chance to batter through him, another shock detonated. He choked on it. "Then the baby isn't…?"

And Larissa delivered another blow, her face contorting, her voice raw. "Oh, God, Faress, no, he *is* Jawad's."

He sagged onto the foot of the bed. If this was Jawad's baby, and she was his widow's sister, that meant…

Larissa scrambled to him on all fours, panicked,

reading where confusion was tossing him, blurted out, "No, no, Faress… He's Claire's!"

He stared at her, overcome, demolished, mute.

She choked on. "Claire and Jawad tried to conceive for years, until they were told it was hopeless. Claire was unable to carry a pregnancy beyond a few weeks. Then Jawad got sick and Claire begged me to be a surrogate mother to their baby. I would have done anything to make Claire and the man she worshipped, and I loved like the brother I never had, happy."

A moment of congealing shock passed before she struggled on.

"Just as we discovered IVF had worked, Jawad died. And his loss killed Claire, literally. She drove her car over a bridge a week after his funeral." She gulped a broken breath. "I—I panicked at first. The soon-to-be single mother of a child who, instead of handing to his parents, I'd have to raise alone when I had a job that had me almost living at the hospital. The first days after Claire died, I broke down, fell prey to all sorts of crazy ideas. Adoption, termination…"

He inhaled a taxed breath. She rushed on, "It was just shock! Those were never options. Then with each hour my concerns died and my feelings for the baby grew. Then as Claire's loss became a reality, I clung to the baby even more as it was all I had left of her. Then I had to sort out Jawad's papers and found out who he was. The rest I've already told you."

Silence throbbed, expanded. Inside Faress's head there was a crashing ocean of realizations. They deluged him, conquered him, paralyzed him. He stared into her abused, anguished eyes.

Could there be relief, *eshg,* like that?

But something was wrong here. Very wrong.

"There could be only one reason you kept silent," he rasped. "You feared you'd have less claim on him as only his next of kin. You feared I'd take control over him. You feared *me*."

"No." She shook, her tresses rioting around her shoulders. "Not you. Not after I got to know you. I feared your father. After—after Ghadah, when I saw him, I—I wanted to leave, without telling you about the baby at all. Then you found out part of the truth, were so angry, so agonized over Jawad, I did fear your reaction if I told you the rest. Then you accused me of coming here to—to trap you, and I defended myself, told you about the baby. When you said you didn't believe it was Jawad's, I was almost relieved, so I'd just get out of here, keep him, knowing I'd tried and failed to give him a family. Then you brought me back and offered

to marry me because you naturally assumed I was the baby's mother…"

She stopped and bit her lip. "I had no illusions that I lost your respect, was afraid if I revealed I had no more claim on the baby than you, you'd take him from me. I was scared he'd end up under your father's thumb, abused like Jawad, raised by hired help while you were too busy to take a real part in his upbringing and…and…"

"And what?" He rose to his feet, struck to his core. "After all we've been through, after you saw me with Jameelah, you still thought I'd leave the baby to my father's mercies and servants' cold care?"

Her whole face shuddered, her swollen eyes squeezed shut. "God, no…Faress, please, I'm sorry…so much was at stake. Then came Jameelah, and I was scared I'd have to leave her, too, if you sent me away. When you didn't mention marriage again, I kept hoping you'd offer me another solution that would make it possible for me to stay and be part of both their lives. I—I don't know what I was hoping for. I was overwhelmed, afraid any step I took in my condition would be the wrong one…

"But—but I've told you now. Now you know I am not genetically his mother, that I withheld the truth, accepted an offer of marriage you made only because you were ignorant of it. And though I did it only for the baby, I'll understand if you don't show me any leniency. But it's not me you should consider here. Please, let me be a part of the baby's life. I am the closest person to his mother he can have. Feeling him growing inside me, I do feel he's mine, yet for being Claire's and Jawad's, for being yours too, he's just *too* precious and I can't bear to think he'd…he'd…"

And she wept as if she'd start weeping blood at any second.

He stared at her, his heart cracking in his chest, his world blackening again. She thought he could take her baby from her? And the baby was all she cared about? And now Jameelah? She'd been hoping he'd forget about his marriage offer?

It could have been an hour when she finally whispered a broken, "Please, Faress…say something."

He sagged on the bed. "*Ya Ullah,* what do you want me to say? That I won't deprive you of your child or Jameelah, or deprive them of you, their surrogate mother? How can you know me so little you even have to ask, to worry?"

Her face flushed with such mortification it caused him physical pain. "Oh, God, I keep making this worse. I believe you're the most noble, caring, protective man on earth, Faress, and all my fears stem from knowing how badly I abused your trust…”

He couldn’t hear that, bear that. “You were protecting your child. To the same end, I’d do far, far more than hide a few facts and consider myself justified.”

Her tears turned off, her eyes flooding with such relief it was equally painful to behold. “Oh, Faress, thank you.”

“*Arjooki*.” He muttered his agonized plea. “*Never* thank me.”

She bit her lip, her eyes almost black now. “Have you thought how I can stay here, be a part of the children’s life? Now there won’t be a marriage…”

“There *will* be a marriage.”

“Oh, so you still intend to…for them…” She nodded, to herself it seemed, like a little girl talking herself into swallowing foul-tasting medicine. “But it won’t be a real one.”

Feeling like he was knowingly stepping into quicksand, he gritted, “It *will* be.”

Larissa jerked at his intensity, her whole being surging with hope. It deflated next second. He meant sex. Of course.

She tried to bring the nauseating tremors arcing through her under control. She would grab at anything he had to offer her, and be thankful for it. She shouldn't even fantasize about more. She should take her own advice, the advice she'd given Jameelah earlier. She was so much luckier than most people. She'd end up having her baby and Jameelah. And the memories of their intimacies when Faress no longer wanted her.

"Just now, I guess you still want me. And I—I want you, too. I only stopped you now, and before, because I couldn't let you make lo—" Her heart stopped for three long beats, aborting the words, and any hope she could ever say them to him. "Uh…h-have sex with me when you didn't know the truth. And when it's over…"

The grimness that had turned his face into stone deepened. "Over?"

"This part of our relationship, I mean…" Oh, God, she couldn't start crying again. Couldn't let him suspect the magnitude of her emotions. He might fear she'd become a liability instead of the helpmeet he thought he was acquiring. She believed it was her reticence so far that made him believe he could trust her to accept her role in his life, the transient place in his bed, that made it possible at all to offer her what he had.

And here she was, laying down the terms of the agreement, delineating how the woman in her would come to life, burn bright with his passion and nearness before she turned to ash and only the doctor and mother remained.

She turned blind eyes around the room, unable to look at him as she propositioned him. "It can be as short as you wish, which, with me pregnant, will probably be very short. And then, after just once you may find out I wasn't worth the trouble after all."

She had to stop. She sounded desperate. As she was. And this wasn't the way to convince him that when he'd had enough of her, she'd let go. She inhaled, strove for her long-lost composure.

There was one last point she wanted to lay to rest.

"About what you said, about me wanting wealth and privileges—I wouldn't know what to do with either. That may sound laughable as I'll be sharing yours to some degree by default, but that's unavoidable as long as I live here for the children's sake. But I won't take anything else. My tastes are simple and my needs are few, and I always made my own living and I wouldn't change that for anything. I—I just want some time with you."

"Just some time," Faress echoed as he moved closer.

She closed her eyes, let his approach permeate

her. Maybe she was deluding herself. Maybe she wouldn't know how to give him up when it was time to do so. Maybe she should tell him to forget it.

She couldn't. She had to be his, be with him, if only once.

She leaned back in bed under the onslaught of arousal, not meeting his eyes so she could bring herself to say this. "I want one night, Faress… tonight. Then I'll retreat from your life, un-until you want another heir. You won't see or hear from me, except as a caregiver of the children, and at work."

Suddenly he snarled, "You want one night? And another when I want another heir? Well, *I* don't."

Her eyes flew up, saw his beloved face working, every muscle in his perfection bulging as if straining under a crushing weight.

"But I thought you wanted me, too…"

"I don't *want* you." This was roared.

Oh, God. He'd just wanted relief, didn't want her specifically. Even that was gone. She wouldn't even have the memories.

Her heart imploding, tears scouring down her cheeks, she dragged the cover around her nakedness, staggered to gather her ruined clothes. "I…I'll just go…"

She turned, blind, finished, and found him

blocking her path, emanating such intensity she swayed.

"Not before you do one thing for me. Explain something. If one night is all you want, what was everything I felt from you all those months? It all made sense when I thought you were Jawad's, your reticence, your resistance. It almost killed me with guilt and jealousy and regret, until I conquered it, knew only that what we share matters. But if this is how you feel, I no longer know if we shared anything. *Ana majnoon?* Am I crazy? Did I imagine all that?"

"Faress…" she choked, reeling.

He kept advancing on her, driving her back until she gratefully felt the wall's support. "Or do you think you can give me all this…uniqueness, then tell it was all for one roll in bed and I wouldn't mind? Why? Because you think I change women as often as I do surgical gloves? Or do you think I'm invincible? I must be a casualty or a child or someone who needs your help for me to deserve your care and caring? I only warranted those when I was devastated and fit those criteria? Now I'm back on my feet, you've moved on to other causes, satisfied that your part is done? Well, it's not. You still have one more mission on my behalf. If you don't need me to exist, then use all that healing and compassion of yours and cure *me* of needing *you* to exist."

She staggered, her heart long burst with every word he'd uttered, everything she felt radiating from him. Everything she'd never let herself fantasize about. Everything she still couldn't let herself begin to believe. "B-but you said you don't want me…"

He smacked his palm against the wall by her head. "I *don't.* Wanting is a grabby, empty, flimsy emotion. And I don't love you either. Love is still too limited and flawed. I don't even worship you. That too can be built on blind, groundless delusion. *Ana aashagek.* Do you know what *eshg* means?" She stared at him, everything inside her still, tears and heartbeats and thought. This was too momentous, too astounding. One single tremor would snap her hold on consciousness. "Everyone says it's all combined, multiplied. But to me it means I have faith in you. That I'd die for you and far worse. That I lust for your every breath and move and inch, crave your well-being and appreciation, depend on your existence and counsel, flourish, *live* with your nearness."

She sagged to her knees, flailing arms hugging his legs, her head resting on one of his thighs, the rising tide of shock and disbelief and elation beyond her ability to process, to withstand.

He felt the same. *He felt the same.*

* * *

Faress stared down at Larissa, his reason and reasons made flesh, kneeling at his feet, flailing as if in a hurricane, whimpers scraping her throat as if in a seizure of prayer, clinging to him as if to a last hope. His immediate impulse was to kneel before *her*, prostrate himself for her mercy. But the sight of her was overpowering, everything flaring from her depths to impact him, psyche and soul, plumbing the reaches of love and devotion. Of *eshg*.

He allowed himself moments, let her storm him, filled himself with her. The cover pooling on her thighs exposing the sweep of a graceful back and flared hips in a pose out of his deepest erotic fantasies, the flames of her hair cascading over one shoulder, raining between his rigid thighs, her face, her working lips almost buried in his painful erection.

He took all he could then snapped, hauled her to bed, covered her with his limbs and lips and debilitating relief and gratitude.

When the extreme of emotion leveled out, she lay in his arms, her eyes on his, and he knew how much of herself she'd been withholding, wondered if he could survive being exposed to her full reality, didn't mind if he didn't.

Her hand trembled on his cheek, in his hair, joy streaming from her eyes. "Will you believe me when I say, me, too, oh, *God*, me, too? All you said? And a whole life full of what I feel for you, and yet more that I'd do for you? You won't ever think I'm exaggerating to…to…?"

"To enslave me? I deserve to be punished for ever for this outburst of insecurity, but I throw myself at your mercy. I was bleeding, was telling myself anything I would listen to, to stop tearing myself apart demanding you."

Indulgence spread her lips, melted him, a tremor of awe in her touch and gaze. "It worked too well on me. I was so afraid that anything that showed you how I feel would be proof you were right. It's still so hard to let go of the dread."

"Let it go, I beg of you. If you're fond of my sanity. I said it but I never believed it. I believed anything you said even when all the evidence was against you. Now my belief is absolute. You've earned it, for ever. So say it, *ya maaboodati*. Have mercy and say it."

Her eyes stilled on his with the solemnity of a revelation, her voice steadying with the firmness of a pledge. "You're beyond hope and dreams, *ya habibi*, and it has nothing to do with who you are. It's what you are, everything I look up to and am awed by. Everything I never thought my children could be blessed enough to have in a father, everything I can only dream my daughter would find a fraction of in the man who'll have her well-being in his safekeeping. You're just too much. I never dared hope you could feel for me anything like I was feeling for you, couldn't believe anyone, let alone me, could aspire to hold your heart. Dying for you would be too little. But I first want to live for you."

And for the first time in his life Faress knew what it meant to feel humble. To feel blessed. He could die now and his life, his happiness would be complete.

He lowered his head, closed his eyes, touched his forehead to hers, groaned, "*Ya rohi*, I had so much to help me become what I am. It's you who are too much, it's I who realize I shouldn't have been so arrogant as to be sure I could hold your heart. But knowing that I do, I have nothing more to ask or expect of this life."

A sob and a convulsive tug brought his lips to hers, inundating him with hunger and more and more confessions.

He wallowed in the deepening certainty for as long as he could stand it. Then emotional confirmation gave way to the demands of the flesh. He imprisoned the hands that branded him, tore her cover away. She lurched with what looked like shyness mixed with arousal, shuddered with the impact of his *eshg*.

He smiled his satisfaction at her reaction before he even touched her, just reading his intentions. And that when she had no idea what he had in store for her yet.

He rained caresses from shoulders to buttocks, a path of torment from gasping lips to begging-for-his-mouth nipples. "I've been waiting for you my whole life, *ya hayati*. I hope you'll forgive the haste when I gulp you down whole. I promise you a lifetime of everything, but now I must devour you."

She twisted in his arms, sat up, grabbing the cover again, looking flustered.

He frowned. "You fear my urgency? You think I'd be rough, wouldn't dissolve you with pleasure?"

Larissa gave a distressed laugh. "If I craved your urgency any more, you'd have to defibrillate me. And I dissolve with pleasure just looking at you. It's just there's one last thing I need to tell you, and I'm not sure how you'll react, as it's really ridiculous, with me being eighteen weeks pregnant, but I'm..." She paused as she struggled with what looked too much like embarrassment. Then, looking as if she was expecting him to start laughing, she burst out, "I'm a virgin."

He stared at her. Just stared.

The heart that had stopped in surprise now began to rumble, like the breakers of his kingdom's seas on its shores in a storm.

She mumbled on, "Since I was a little girl, I've always wanted love. Then Claire found Jawad and I was more adamant I either had the same, that totality of desire and understanding and commitment, or I didn't want anything at all. Then I thought having their child would be…" Her color rose, her eyes fluctuated among half a dozen distressed hues. "I don't know how to say this so it won't sound stupid, but it seemed like an equally worthy cause to…to offer my body to."

Faress moved, measured, controlled. Otherwise he would ravage her until he'd finished her. That would come later.

Now he took the midnight blue cover she held to her body like a shield, and slowly, so slowly, dragged it down.

"I knew it." He laid her back, spread her, took in every shudder as his voracity singed her. "In my blood, my bones. Your flesh, your essence called to me, from that first moment, demanded mine, decreed my surrender, predestined my enslavement, pledged yours. Now you'll have everything, your goal of sharing your first intimacy, all our intimacies, in the absoluteness of *eshg*, then you'll have this most treasured baby. And I'll have you both, miracles from *Ullah* I'll live my life striving to deserve. And with Jameelah and any more children you can give me, I'll have the world and beyond."

Larissa was shaking so hard her teeth rattled. "Faress, please, I can't breathe…" And it did seem she couldn't. She was gasping, looking faint. "My heart…it'll stop…if I don't have you, if you don't take me. Don't torment me any more…please, please, now…"

"*Umrek, ya rohi*, command me, and I'm yours." He came over her, parted her trembling thighs, slipped a careful finger inside her, felt the truth of her words. She was flowing for him. She thrashed, attempted to clamp him to her. He soothed her frenzy, trying to mask his own, rein it in, took her buttocks in one hand, tilted her to him as his other roamed her, in wonder, in ownership. He brought his shaft to her body's scorching entrance, rested there, struggling with the elemental need to plunge, seek her depths, go home.

Gritting his teeth, he began to invade her, her trust, her hunger, her beauty open before him, her constant pleas a continuous current fusing his insides.

The feel of her attempting to open to accept him, knowing that he'd cause her pain before he gave her pleasure, the concept of finally merging with her, and that she *had* been made for him, had waited to find him, made him almost weep.

"Please, Faress, make me yours…" she wailed.

There was only so much he could take.

He surrendered to her, to a fraction of the need, pushed into her, going blind with the burst of pleasure, the tightness of her velvet vise enveloping him. The tears he'd never thought he'd shed after Ghadah and Jawad welling in his eyes at feeling the hotness of her blood mix with that of her arousal, at the measure of the gift she was bestowing on him, at her attempts to smother the sharpness of her pain.

He stilled in her depths as she arched off the bed with the shock of his invasion, shuddering, praying the worst of it would pass quickly. "*Samheeni, ya rohi.*" He panted his agitation, adjusted his position to maximize her comfort, roamed her ripeness with soothing, worshipping hands and lips. "Forgive me…I'll make it up to you in a lifetime of pleasures…"

"No, no…" she moaned, rigidity draining out of her beloved body. "I've waited my life for this, for you, but never dreamed, *never*…" Her fingers dug into his chest, his shoulders, bringing him down to her, forcing him to stroke deeper into her. She cried out this time, a hot sharp sound that tore a growl out of him. He heard exultation mixed with the pain now, his heart booming with relief, pride.

She thrashed her head, never taking her eyes off his, letting him see every sensation ripping through her, her flaming hair, her paleness brightening with her rising pleasure, burning up the darkness she lay on.

"You're magnificent inside me," she panted, her voice smoky, the exhilaration thickening it sending another tidal wave of arousal crashing through his body. "Never knew so much pleasure existed. Give me all of you, *ya habibi*, love me, take me."

"Aih, ya rohi, et'mataii..." He rumbled to her to take her fill of pleasure as he began to feed her hunger more of him, struggling as the slide inside her gripping heat sliced through him, still afraid she couldn't accommodate all of him. He watched in awe and receding sanity as she accepted more of him, arching, offering, abandoned. Then she was weeping, her cries rising as she snatched for him, seeking his lips in another exercise of abandon, her core throbbing around his invasion, pouring a surplus of welcome, demanding more of him. He couldn't believe she'd reached fever pitch so soon. But, then, so had he. And he had to obey her.

He withdrew then plunged, burying himself all

the way inside her. Her scream ripped through him as her body convulsed. Then she shattered around him, her fit shredding her screams. The knowledge that he was pleasuring her, fulfilling her, boiled his seed in his loins, her wrenching tightness tearing his answering orgasm from depths he'd never known existed.

With the wish that one day his seed would take root in her womb too, produce another child of their own flesh and love, he jetted inside her, causing her paroxysm to spike. One detonation of ecstasy after another rocked him, her, held them in a closed circuit of over-stimulation, their eyes locked together in shock at sensations so sharp it felt they'd cause lasting damage. They plateaued until she was sobbing, he grunting, clinging together, dissolving in each other, at the mercy of a merciless first.

When he felt his heart would never restart, the convulsions of release gave way to the flooding warmth and weakness of satiation. He felt her melt around him, awe and cell-deep satisfaction glowing on her face.

"*Marati,*" he rumbled against her lips as he twisted around, bringing her lying on top of him, maintaining their merging.

"Your woman, yes...oh, yes..." Her voice was

different, awareness-laden, smug, overcome. She opened her lips over his heart. It almost rammed out of his ribs for a direct kiss. Then she bit into him, delicate, devouring. *"Rejjali…?"*

"Ya Ullah, bedoon shak," he groaned, feeling she'd uprooted his heart, taken it into her possession. "No doubt ever, your man. And everything else you need me to be, for ever."

She raised her head, her hair raining all over his chest, in her eyes everything he'd live for from now on. "I knew the first moment I saw you that my body had been made to sing when yours was near. It was like I'd turned into a living tuning fork with your vibe the frequency that sets me off. But I still had no idea what I've been missing. Now I am kicking myself I didn't surrender to you the first moment you wanted me."

He stroked her, turned her to lie beside him, in more comfort. "It wouldn't have been like that at first. This…cataclysm we just shared was all emotional, and we needed to go through all that we did to achieve this pinnacle."

She gave him such a smile, no inhibitions, no uncertainties, awakened, gaining in confidence. She'd become annihilating when she realized her full power. He couldn't wait to be devastated.

"I achieved that emotional pinnacle a long time

ago," she whispered, between kisses all over his chest. "I should have snatched at you then. But my excuse is I had no idea it could be anything like this. No imagination or fantasy could have done what you did to me, what you gave me justice. But if it was a fraction as life-changing for you as it was for me, and you knew it would be, how did you not take me long ago? What's your excuse?"

"My excuse is that I had no idea it could be like this. I only had experience with sex…" She moaned, bit into him, punishing him for daring to have shared his body in meaningless physical release with others. He'd let her punish him, long and elaborately. "I had no idea what love, what intimacy, what dark, raging, blinding, transfiguring passion can be like. What the woman I was created for would do to me with her hunger, her surrender." She shuddered, more bliss seeping from her eyes to splash his chest. He bit one nipple, the body that hadn't subsided surging to full need as she blossomed under his hunger, undulating in a sinuous dance of urgency and demand and submission.

"Faress, *habibi*, take me again. Don't make me wait."

"You're sore. You can't take me again."

"I can. I want the pain and anything else. I just

want to experience everything with you, feel your weight on me, feel you inside me, stretching me, dominating me, until I'm finished, complete. Just take me, come inside me, fill me, *ya habibi*."

In answer to her pleas, Faress sprang out of bed in one impossible movement, then bent to carry her as if she weighed no more than ten pounds, not her now substantial one-forty.

She cried out and he gave her a devilish smile. "All good things, all mind-blowing pleasure come to she who waits."

He was taking her to his *hammam*! She nearly fainted with the surge of images and the pangs of hunger they elicited.

He strode into the otherworldly hall, placed her on the glowing white marble platform, making her feel he was placing a priceless work of art on a pedestal. He suckled on each nipple, then gestured to her to stay in place as he walked away.

He came back with steam already billowing around him, a colossus of virile beauty stepping from the shroud of myth and time, and amazingly, unbelievably, hers.

The half-light worshipped endless shoulders and chest, muscled arms, defined abdomen and muscled thighs flanking a manhood whose sight rattled her with arousal and amazement that she'd been able to accommodate all that power and potency.

She lay back, struck mute, her mouth watering, her insides cramping, dizzy with the aftershocks of the transfiguring experience in his arms. The pleasure had been enough to overcome her, but the concept, the reality of his possession, the force of his passion, the heights of his generosity…! She'd metamorphosed in those minutes. She'd become a new creature, truly his.

In her recklessness she'd demanded him again. She had no idea if she'd survive those heights again or, as she suspected, something even fiercer, more uninhibited.

He came to stand over her, the purity of his emotions emblazoned on his face. "I claimed you, *ya galbi*," he said, raggedly. "Gave myself to you." Suddenly his solemn lips turned wicked. "And now…I pleasure you."

And as his hands slid over her now slick flesh, seeking her secrets, finding triggers she hadn't known she had, teasing, igniting, life expectancy became a serious issue.

CHAPTER TWELVE

FROM the depths of Faress-filled dreams, dreams that had failed to even mimic the wonder of him, the magic he'd exposed her to, Larissa opened her lips to his reality, to his cosseting, his ownership. She surfaced from the luxury of their mouths mating to the face, the smile, the reason of everything she'd wake up every morning for, as long as she lived.

"Aroah sabah fi hayati, ya hayati," he murmured, caught her answering delight in his lips again before moving his possession down to her core, tasting and teasing her in another soothing invasion, what he'd exposed her to a dozen times during the night.

"I need no more healing, Faress, just come inside me…" Her sobs choked on another heaving climax.

He came up after completing her pleasure, satisfaction and pride blazing, hunger so ferocious it cleaved into her. But she knew, no matter how she begged him, he wouldn't take her again. He was determined her next time would be pure bliss.

He drowned her in his embrace, his hardness against her side betraying the magnitude of his need, his control. He sighed. "The most incredible morning of my life, for certain, my life."

"Ahebbak, ya habibi, aashagak." She surged in his arms, sought his lips, his treasures, greedy, awed hands seeking his potency as she invaded the fount of his taste with all her fervor, moved beyond her ability to contain it, her heart pouring into him. "That you exist, that I am yours…*aahen ya habibi…*"

He surrendered to her ministrations, her ownership, magnanimous with his demonstrations, his hypnotic eyes never leaving hers as he let her see how much, how far in her power he was, roaring his surrender, convulsing in his pleasure.

Afterwards they lay stunned yet again at the depth of their connection, its unending promise.

Suddenly trepidation started to seep through her nerves.

This was too incredible. Could life offer something of that magnitude and not exact equal and opposite payback?

Then they heard the buzz.

She felt Faress stiffen, the eyes drenching her in

eshg draining of all expression. She choked on her heart. "What is it?"

He took her trembling lips, but it wasn't a kiss. It was a pledge. It scared her even more.

"It's nothing you should worry about, *ya rohi*," he said. "Go to work if you like today. I'll catch up as soon as I'm done." Then, with a final caress, he left her arms.

In minutes he was dressed and gone.

It was the king. He'd summoned Faress. She'd put two and two together after he'd gone.

Going crazy wondering what was going on, Larissa decided to go to work. Even if she wasn't up to working today, her team would keep her sane until she saw Faress again.

It was after breakfast, during another debate between Helal and Anika, the other blazing, if decidedly different in tone romance developing during the project, that she learned some vital truths, about Jawad's history and the current situation.

"After your all-knowing assertions last time, Helal…" Anika cocked an eyebrow at him "…I did some research. And it isn't true that a male child of Prince Jawad's would have become crown prince instead of Dr. Faress. You should do your homework before you shoot your mouth off."

"Oh?" Helal dropped beside her, his eyes promising retribution. "And what new 'facts' have you uncovered? When nobody in the kingdom talks about why Prince Jawad was supplanted by Prince Faress as crown prince?"

Anika smirked. "I told you you're not talking to real Bidalyans, Helal. The ones I talked to told me it hadn't been made public, but everyone knows the king was enraged when Jawad refused to enter into the state marriage he'd arranged for him, insisted on marrying the woman he loved. The king stripped him of his titles and wealth, even threatened to 'deal' with the woman who presumed to seduce his heir, hoping it would bring him to his senses. But what Jawad did was disappear. When the king failed to locate him and drag him back, in a fit of rage over his son's insubordination he issued another royal decree that Jawad and his line would forever be denied right of succession."

Larissa squeezed her eyes, hot shame and mortification clogging her throat. The baby had been denied all his rights. This meant Faress was actually reinstating them by claiming him as his. And she'd been so stupid, so suspicious. She'd doubted his intentions, no matter how fleetingly.

"If this is true, Ani," Patrick rumbled, "then let's

hope Dr. Faress doesn't anger the old man and accept the marriage of state I hear he's pushing down his throat."

"Logic says that even if he doesn't," Tom interjected reasonably, "the king can't disown him, too. He's out of heirs. Princess Ghadah only had one daughter."

"Logic? You clearly know nothing about the old fossil," Helal scoffed. "If Prince Faress thwarts him, he'd throw the succession to any cousin. Probably the most inept one, just to spite Faress."

Larissa stopped listening. Suspicion mushroomed in her system, congealing to a heart-snatching certainty in seconds.

Faress was risking his birthright to have her and the baby.

And she knew what that pledge before he'd left had been. He'd been telling her nothing would stop him from having them.

She didn't know what she said to her team as she ran out. She only knew she had to stop Faress from throwing everything away.

She tried to reach him on his cellphone as she raced to the king's palace, to no avail.

On arrival, she was received with all the deference a royal guest would receive. It had to be on Faress's orders.

But it was too late. Faress was already with the king.

She begged the one who seemed like head of security to transmit an urgent message to Faress. Hesitating to interrupt his king's private audience with his son, yet bound by that son's orders to answer her every request, he consented to try.

Minutes passed until she felt she'd start running through the palace, yelling for Faress, any second.

The man suddenly reappeared. "Dr. McPherson. You're to be admitted into the king's presence."

"But I just need to talk to Prince Faress…" she faltered.

The man bowed his head. "You're summoned to the king's presence by *Somow'w'el Ameer* Faress's orders."

She staggered behind him in chaos. Why had Faress done that? She didn't want to see that man, and more so with every step through his palace's impossible opulence, pompous and extravagant where Faress's was tasteful and prosperous.

Her stomach roiling with anxiety, she walked into the king's stateroom. The first thing she saw was Faress, striding towards her, his eyes fierce, his jaw set. She had no idea how she stopped herself from throwing herself into his arms.

Acutely aware of his father's presence, his rage, her chaos spiked when Faress embraced her.

"I'm loath for you to witness this," he murmured against her lips, "but I couldn't leave you outside."

"Is this the harlot come to take my one remaining offspring?"

This couldn't be the voice of a man. It was the roar of a wounded monster. Larissa started in Faress's arms, felt him stiffen as he whirled around.

"Have a care, Father," Faress rumbled, his voice as low and as frightening as his father's explosive fury. It gave the older man pause.

Then his rage spiked as he stormed towards them, as big as Faress, bulkier. He must have been as handsome once, but his volatile ruthlessness furrowed his good looks, made him forbidding, sinister.

"I know who your harlot is, Faress," the king raved. "Did *you*? Or did she con you like her harlot of a sister conned Jawad?" At uttering Jawad's name something crazed came into his eyes. He roared, "Jawad. Dead. Ghadah. Dead. And this…this…" He made a snatch at her. Her heart hit the base of her throat. Faress's lightning move intercepted his father. As she staggered out of the man's reach, Faress grabbed his father's arms, overpowered him with steady power until the older man stood grunting with effort, shaking with frustration, pain and rage.

"I know what you're going through, Father…" Faress started, a pained look on his face at his father's devastation.

"You know nothing," the king snarled, sounding even more deranged. "They were just your siblings. They were my firstborn, my hope, my little girl, the balm of my soul. Tell me you know what I'm going through when you bury two children."

"I know what you're going through," Faress insisted. "I almost lost everyone I hold dear yesterday, and I know I would have been driven to extremes if it had come to pass. But you're the one who deprived us of Jawad, so own up to it."

After a long wrestling look between father and son, the king relinquished what he knew was a losing match, turned his disturbed and disturbing gaze on Larissa.

"You… I'm not letting you take my only remaining son. I'm throwing you out of Bidalya." He turned his rabid eyes on Faress. "And you had better not intervene."

Faress held his father's gaze and weighed his options. He'd never seen him like this. The certainty of Jawad's loss, his guilt over his role in it all was tampering with his sanity. If he told his father Larissa was carrying all they had left of Jawad he might relent. But with his father so unstable, he couldn't risk him going into another fit of royal retribution, insisting on still disowning Jawad's son as well, or, worse, snatching him away from Larissa and banning her from seeing him ever again. There were no options really. His father, though he bled for him, had forfeited his right to his family.

"Oh, I wouldn't intervene, Father." He felt Larissa's start. He grated on, "I'd only leave with her. Larissa isn't only the woman I love, she's my wife, already pregnant with my heir. I've only been waiting for the proper time to take our vows again in the Bidalyan tradition, wanted you to be part of a family that will give you a new daughter and a grandson. But you can cling to your irrationalities. Like Jawad, my first loyalty and duty is to the woman who owns my heart. Exile her and you'll never see me again either."

"Then get out of my sight, both of you," the king thundered. "Out of my kingdom."

Faress merely gave his father a small bow, wrapped his arm around her and walked her out.

* * *

Larissa remained in shock all through the rush to the palace to collect Jameelah then to the airport to board one of Faress's private jets.

They were in the air and the bewildered if excited Jameelah had fallen asleep in one of the jet's two bedroom suites when Larissa finally caught Faress between his continuous phone calls.

"I can't let you do this to yourself or to Bidalya," she blurted out. "You were born to be king and I won't let you sacrifice yourself for me and my baby."

He pulled her onto his lap, nuzzled her neck. "I was born to be yours, your man and the father of our children. I was born to fight to my last breath for you. You're already my wife before God. I don't care about being Bidalya's crown prince or future king. I only want to be your knight and king of your heart."

She squirmed, tried to slow down her descent into his thrall. This had to be resolved. "You'll always be that. But you don't have to give up anything to have me. I'm yours for ever, and will live for the time when you can be with us." He just shook his head and she got desperate. "You can't throw away your birthright like Jawad did!"

His gaze stilled on her until she felt he'd penetrated her down to her marrow. Then he asked, "Did it ever seem to you that Jawad was unhappy?

In the years of his marriage to your sister, did you feel he had any regrets?"

She closed her eyes, knowing he'd cornered her.

"Not for a second," she admitted thickly. "Through the trials of infertility and terminal illness, I never saw a man happier or more in love than Jawad."

"You're *looking* at that man." His voice was certainty itself. "But unlike Jawad, I have extensive wealth and status independent of my royal position. We'll go wherever we want, set up our humanitarian operations, our hospitals and research centers and be productive and happy together for the rest of our lives."

Everything he said humbled her, made her delirious with elation. But she was still oppressed at the massive privileges he was throwing away to be with her.

She tried again. "*Habibi*, I'll give my life, every minute of it, to make you happy, to deserve your love and faith. But you don't have to marry me. Your love is all I want from life…"

His mouth, passionate and overriding, silenced her. Then he murmured, "You're having all of me. For ever. Any objections?"

Larissa could no longer find any.

Drowning in his arms, she came out of her haze

of happiness to the sound of the jet landing. A glance outside the jet confirmed one thing. They'd landed back in Bidalya!

It had to be the king's doing.

Next moment, her deduction was confirmed. The king appeared on the screens of Faress's video conferencing facility.

The king looked haggard, defeated. He started immediately as soon as Faress opened the channel.

"I can't lose another son, *ya bnai*. And Bidalya can't lose the man best suited to be its king. I want you back and I want you to start the restructuring plans you've been proposing."

Then he was gone.

Faress stared at the blank screen for a while. Then he turned to Larissa, serious, intense. Her heart thumped.

He exhaled. "My father really knows how to offer bait when he wants to. He just offered me what I thought he'd never agree to. To start reorganizing the rule in the kingdom now, in his lifetime, so that by the time I come to reign, the monarchy will have far less power and I will have far less to do as king, so that I can continue being a surgeon."

She was stunned. "Oh, God, Faress. That's huge. And so exciting. And scary."

"Indeed. And I'll need all the help I can get to organize my time. And who better than you? You showed me new levels of time efficiency, and efficiency in general. Will you be my personal advisor, my official right hand in all things medical?"

Larissa flung herself at him, took his lips, rained kisses in a fever over his beloved face. "I'll be anything you want. Anything. I'll take on the whole world, take the most grueling tests, perform the impossible, for ever."

He took over until she was trembling, writhing.

"You already did that and then some, *ya rohi*," he growled, then swung her in his arms, heading for the other bedroom. "Not in a hurry to leave the jet, are you?" She shook her head frantically. He chuckled as he locked the door behind them.

A long time later, they were moaning their completion, watching stars outside the window twinkling in the inky sky, when he suddenly groaned.

"You make me forget the world." He rose over her. "But we must make plans for our wedding. When would you like to have it?"

Snuggling into the heaven and haven of his arms, she chuckled. "Any time before I'm in labor would be good."

EPILOGUE

FARESS managed that, barely.

Because of the changes Faress had to put in place before the wedding took place, Larissa shocked the world by showing up eight months pregnant in the internationally broadcast marriage ceremony, and in a conservative country like Bidalya to boot.

Bidalya's crown prince and the proud and magnificent groom in traditional ceremonial garb rose from their matrimonial *kousha* and announced that this was a belated public ceremony, that their marriage had taken place a year ago, and that there would be another ceremony on the birth of their first child. He proclaimed that both days would become national holidays.

Then he turned, winked at the distraught with excitement Jameelah, before coming to stand above Larissa.

Suddenly, he knelt. The crowds went wild.

Ecstatically wrecked, Larissa barely managed

not to fall at his feet in a heap, remembering the decorum she was supposed to show as a princess of Bidalya. Faress produced an anklet right out of Ali Baba's treasures, took her green silk moccasin-like clad foot, raised it, placed a fervent kiss on her exposed flesh. The crowds roared like a raging storm with approval.

Looking into her drenched eyes, he whispered, for her ears only, "*Maaboodati*, my goddess, I give you everything that I am." Then he snapped the anklet in place.

He stood up, pulled her to her wobbly feet, supported her swaying, heavily pregnant body all through endless, hyper-charged minutes of waving to the crowds.

Finally the public celebrations started, and he seated her, sat down beside her, pride and ever-increasing *eshg* blazing in his obsidian eyes.

Giggling, going to pieces, Larissa gasped, "The way we left things, those two holidays you proclaimed will be too close together. Little Jawad is probably days from making his entrance into the world."

Faress took her clammy hand, kissed it. "And next year at the same time, we may even have a little Claire to crowd the month with one more national holiday."

Choking up even more, Larissa tried not to break down with happiness. "In the interests of interspersing those, we have to plan a bit. I'd love to have a winter baby."

"You can have everything you want," he declared, his eyes vowing. "Whenever you want it, and a baby in each season. I want to fill my world with little replicas of you."

And Larissa shocked the world again.

She threw herself at him, her emotions and passion and gratitude for all that he was boiling over in an all-the-way kiss.

She dimly heard the roaring of the crowds reaching a crescendo. And realized.

Not only were public displays of affection frowned upon here, this was Faress's personal inclination. He'd kissed her hand and foot in tenderness and chivalry, but the kiss she was giving him was right out of their erotically abandoned encounters.

She'd compromised his image, started her life as his princess proving how unsuitable she was for the role…

She jerked out of his arms. "Oh, God, I'm sorry Faress…"

He pulled her back, his laughter the very sound of delight and arousal. Then he kissed her again.

This time he really gave the crowds something for their eyes to pop over.

When he at last let go of her lips, he kept her ensconced in his embrace, an ecstatic mass of agitation. And *eshg*.

Tilting her face up to him to let him see it all, she saw his own *eshg* in his eyes as he murmured, "This is the…"

"This was the best wedding gift you could have given me, *ya roh galbi*. Showing me in front of the whole world that nothing matters but me. Worry about behaving with all the decorum of a princess in public…tomorrow. Now let's give the world a royal wedding that will make history."

And he took her lips again.

MEDICAL™

Large Print

Titles for the next six months…

November

NURSE BRIDE, BAYSIDE WEDDING	Gill Sanderson
BILLIONAIRE DOCTOR, ORDINARY NURSE	Carol Marinelli
THE SHEIKH SURGEON'S BABY	Meredith Webber
THE OUTBACK DOCTOR'S SURPRISE BRIDE	Amy Andrews
A WEDDING AT LIMESTONE COAST	Lucy Clark
THE DOCTOR'S MEANT-TO-BE MARRIAGE	Janice Lynn

December

SINGLE DAD SEEKS A WIFE	Melanie Milburne
HER FOUR-YEAR BABY SECRET	Alison Roberts
COUNTRY DOCTOR, SPRING BRIDE	Abigail Gordon
MARRYING THE RUNAWAY BRIDE	Jennifer Taylor
THE MIDWIFE'S BABY	Fiona McArthur
THE FATHERHOOD MIRACLE	Margaret Barker

January

VIRGIN MIDWIFE, PLAYBOY DOCTOR	Margaret McDonagh
THE REBEL DOCTOR'S BRIDE	Sarah Morgan
THE SURGEON'S SECRET BABY WISH	Laura Iding
PROPOSING TO THE CHILDREN'S DOCTOR	Joanna Neil
EMERGENCY: WIFE NEEDED	Emily Forbes
ITALIAN DOCTOR, FULL-TIME FATHER	Dianne Drake

MEDICAL™

Large Print

February

THEIR MIRACLE BABY	Caroline Anderson
THE CHILDREN'S DOCTOR AND THE SINGLE MUM	Lilian Darcy
THE SPANISH DOCTOR'S LOVE-CHILD	Kate Hardy
PREGNANT NURSE, NEW-FOUND FAMILY	Lynne Marshall
HER VERY SPECIAL BOSS	Anne Fraser
THE GP'S MARRIAGE WISH	Judy Campbell

March

SHEIKH SURGEON CLAIMS HIS BRIDE	Josie Metcalfe
A PROPOSAL WORTH WAITING FOR	Lilian Darcy
A DOCTOR, A NURSE: A LITTLE MIRACLE	Carol Marinelli
TOP-NOTCH SURGEON, PREGNANT NURSE	Amy Andrews
A MOTHER FOR HIS SON	Gill Sanderson
THE PLAYBOY DOCTOR'S MARRIAGE PROPOSAL	Fiona Lowe

April

A BABY FOR EVE	Maggie Kingsley
MARRYING THE MILLIONAIRE DOCTOR	Alison Roberts
HIS VERY SPECIAL BRIDE	Joanna Neil
CITY SURGEON, OUTBACK BRIDE	Lucy Clark
A BOSS BEYOND COMPARE	Dianne Drake
THE EMERGENCY DOCTOR'S CHOSEN WIFE	Molly Evans

1008 LP 2P P2 Medical